In a German Pension

In a German Pension

Katherine Mansfield

ET REMOTISSIMA PROPE

100 PAGES

100 PAGES
Published by Hesperus Press Limited
4 Rickett Street, London SW6 1RU
www.hesperuspress.com

First published in 1911
This edition first published by Hesperus Press Limited, 2003

Designed and typeset by Fraser Muggeridge
Printed in the United Arab Emirates by Oriental Press

ISBN: 1-84391-041-1

CONTENTS

FOREWORD

A young woman sits in the garden of a German pension in the first decade of the last century trying to write a poem. Dissatisfied with her imagery she eavesdrops on a pair of lovers (a student from Bonn and the sister of a baroness), hoping she will hear something she can filch. The student, she understands, must do his utmost to woo the high-born lady: 'He had hitherto relied upon three scars and a ribbon to produce an effect, but the sister of a baroness demanded more than these.' The young poetess has high hopes. A pair of hands, she hears, is like 'white lilies lying on the pool of your black dress.' This sounds promising. Next, the prospect of a kiss is raised, but must be dismissed: '"...you know I am suffering from severe nasal catarrh, and I dare not risk giving it to you. Sixteen times last night did I count myself sneezing. And three different handkerchiefs."' Even worse, over the page we find a case of mistaken identity: the lady in question is the baroness' dressmaker.

Katherine Mansfield's was one of the first modern voices. She breezes over to Europe from her birthplace, New Zealand, and lets fresh air into rooms from which the aroma rises of camphor, tea, sausage, dusty flowers, stale eau de Cologne. The stories that follow under the title *In a German Pension* were the first she published, in 1911. She wrote them while recuperating in Germany, apparently after a miscarriage and a short, violent marriage. Some are first-person satirical studies of her fellow-guests in a boarding house, others walk through the town and into the bedrooms of the houses, eavesdropping on childbirth, an attempted rape, a child smothering another child. Stifled lives, close, overheated rooms. What would chill them was the coming war. In Mansfield's stories the Germans and the English bicker over their cultural superiority. The correct method of making a pot of tea provokes a row that threatens to boil over.

Mansfield was funny, as her contemporaries D.H. Lawrence and Virginia Woolf were not: in 'Frau Fischer' the narrator is forced to invent a seafaring husband to avoid the enquiries of her fellow-guests about her personal situation; her creation becomes so fanciful that the more she embroiders, the more her credulous enquirer believes her: 'This husband that I had created for the benefit of Frau Fischer became in her hands so substantial a figure that I could no longer see myself sitting on a rock with seaweed in my hair, awaiting that phantom ship for which all women love to suppose they hunger. Rather I saw myself pushing a perambulator up the gangway and counting up the missing buttons on my husband's uniform jacket... I decided to wreck my virgin conception and send him down somewhere off Cape Horn.'

She seems to specialise in found speech, a kind of Alan Bennett of the Edwardian German drawing-room, and records it with a young woman's glee, and I'm reminded of Jane Austen, but the narrator's precarious position in this world makes her more like the Jean Rhys who wrote of women who sit in a room waiting for a cheque from a lover so they can buy a dress to enable them to go to a restaurant and find another lover. Between marriage and prostitution there are limited opportunities for those without a trust fund. Mansfield's stories are full of these women of the early years of the century, teetering between domination by their menfolk and the first tentative steps towards independence. In 'The Advanced Lady' a woman in a white gown and her hair loose (shades of Isadora Duncan?) amazes the fellow-guests with the announcement that she is writing a book: '"Yes, it is a novel – upon the Modern Woman. For this seems to me the woman's hour."' It was and it wasn't. Mansfield was writing during the suffragette period. If women could not even vote what hope was there for personal liberation? Her female characters are, in turns, vapid, vain, pompous, timid, but above all bourgeois. Suffering occurs behind closed doors, out of sight, as sexually ignorant new wives submit in terror to the brutal advances of bridegrooms, and a mother gives birth in an upstairs room while below her husband has a neurotic moment and imagines he has suffered.

Who and what is a woman to be? asks Viola in 'The Swing of the Pendulum'. Sitting in her room in the German pension, without the money for the rent, she weighs her options. Her suitor, Casimir, and his future promise as a dull, serious and unsuccessful husband? Independence? Doesn't want it; she feels herself to have been born for 'ease and any amount of nursing in the lap of luxury'. The life of a great courtesan? She doesn't know how to go about it. Then a knock at the door, an attractive stranger, 'he looked as though he could order a magnificent dinner... How hungry she had been for the nearness of someone like that – who knew nothing at all about her – and made no demands – but just lived.' There are hungers and there are appetites. The stranger finds a woman alone in a room, flirtatious, unprotected, and 'slipped one arm round her body, and drew her towards him – like a bar of iron across her back – that arm.'

In a later short story ('Bliss', published after the war), Mansfield would ask: 'What can you do if you are thirty and, turning the corner of your own street, you are overcome, suddenly, by a feeling of bliss – absolute bliss! – as though you'd suddenly swallowed a bright piece of that late afternoon sun and it burned in your bosom, sending out a little shower of sparks into every particle, into every finger and toe?…'

The girl in the pension longed for bliss; she was offered sauerkraut or rape. The assault on both was to be Mansfield's (too short) life's work.

– *Linda Grant, 2003*

In a German Pension

Germans at Meat

Bread soup was placed upon the table.

'Ah,' said the Herr Rat, leaning upon the table as he peered into the tureen, 'that is what I need. My *Magen*[1] has not been in order for several days. Bread soup, and just the right consistency. I am a good cook myself' – he turned to me.

'How interesting,' I said, attempting to infuse just the right amount of enthusiasm into my voice.

'Oh yes – when one is not married it is necessary. As for me, I have had all I wanted from women without marriage.' He tucked his napkin into his collar and blew upon his soup as he spoke. 'Now at nine o'clock I make myself an English breakfast, but not much. Four slices of bread, two eggs, two slices of cold ham, one plate of soup, two cups of tea – that is nothing to you.'

He asserted the fact so vehemently that I had not the courage to refute it.

All eyes were suddenly turned upon me. I felt I was bearing the burden of the nation's preposterous breakfast – I, who drank a cup of coffee while buttoning my blouse in the morning.

'Nothing at all,' cried Herr Hoffmann from Berlin. '*Ach*, when I was in England in the morning I used to eat.' He turned up his eyes and his moustache, wiping the soup drippings from his coat and waistcoat.

'Do they really eat so much?' asked Fräulein Stiegelauer. 'Soup and baker's bread and pig's flesh, and tea and coffee and stewed fruit, and honey and eggs, and cold fish and kidneys, and hot fish and liver? All the ladies eat, too, especially the ladies?'

'Certainly. I myself have noticed it, when I was living in a hotel in Leicester Square,' cried the Herr Rat. 'It was a good hotel, but they could not make tea – now –'

'Ah, that's one thing I *can* do,' said I, laughing brightly. 'I can make very good tea. The great secret is to warm the teapot.'

'Warm the teapot,' interrupted the Herr Rat, pushing away his soup plate. 'What do you warm the teapot for? Ha! ha! that's very good! One does not eat the teapot, I suppose?'

He fixed his cold blue eyes upon me with an expression which suggested a thousand premeditated invasions.

'So that is the great secret of your English tea? All you do is to warm the teapot.'

I wanted to say that was only the preliminary canter, but could not translate it, and so was silent.

The servant brought in veal, with sauerkraut and potatoes.

'I eat sauerkraut with great pleasure,' said the Traveller from North Germany, 'but now I have eaten so much of it that I cannot retain it. I am immediately forced to –'

'A beautiful day,' I cried, turning to Fräulein Stiegelauer. 'Did you get up early?'

'At five o'clock I walked for ten minutes in the wet grass. Again in bed. At half-past five I fell asleep, and woke at seven, when I made an "overbody" washing! Again in bed. At eight o'clock I had a cold-water poultice, and at half-past eight I drank a cup of mint tea. At nine I drank some malt coffee, and began my "cure". Pass me the sauerkraut, please. You do not eat it?'

'No, thank you. I still find it a little strong.'

'Is it true,' asked the Widow, picking her teeth with a hairpin as she spoke, 'that you are a vegetarian?'

'Why, yes; I have not eaten meat for three years.'

'Im-possible! Have you any family?'

'No.'

'There now, you see, that's what you're coming to! Who ever heard of having children upon vegetables? It is not possible. But you never have large families in England now; I suppose you are too busy with your suffragetting. Now I have had nine children, and they are all alive, thank God. Fine, healthy babies – though after the first one was born I had to –'

'How *wonderful*!' I cried.

'Wonderful,' said the Widow contemptuously, replacing the hairpin in the knob which was balanced on the top of her head. 'Not at all! A friend of mine had four at the same time. Her husband was so pleased he gave a supper party and had them placed on the table. Of course she was very proud.'

'Germany,' boomed the Traveller, biting round a potato which he had speared with his knife, 'is the home of the Family.'

Followed an appreciative silence.

The dishes were changed for beef, redcurrants and spinach. They wiped their forks upon black bread and started again.

'How long are you remaining here?' asked the Herr Rat.

'I do not know exactly. I must be back in London in September.'

'Of course you will visit München?'

'I am afraid I shall not have time. You see, it is important not to break into my "cure".'

'But you *must* go to München. You have not seen Germany if you have not been to München. All the Exhibitions, all the Art and Soul life of Germany are in München. There is the Wagner Festival in August, and Mozart and a Japanese collection of pictures – and there is the beer! You do not know what good beer is until you have been to München. Why, I see fine ladies every afternoon, but fine ladies, I tell you, drinking glasses so high.' He measured a good washstand pitcher in height, and I smiled.

'If I drink a great deal of München beer I sweat so,' said Herr Hoffmann. 'When I am here, in the fields or before my baths, I sweat, but I enjoy it; but in the town it is not at all the same thing.'

Prompted by the thought, he wiped his neck and face with his dinner napkin and carefully cleaned his ears.

A glass dish of stewed apricots was placed upon the table.

'Ah, fruit!' said Fräulein Stiegelauer, 'that is so necessary to health. The doctor told me this morning that the more fruit I could eat the better.'

She very obviously followed the advice.

Said the Traveller: 'I suppose you are frightened of an invasion, too, eh? Oh, that's good. I've been reading all about your English play in a newspaper. Did you see it?'

'Yes.' I sat upright. 'I assure you we are not afraid.'

'Well, then, you ought to be,' said the Herr Rat. 'You have got no army at all – a few little boys with their veins full of nicotine poisoning.'

'Don't be afraid,' Herr Hoffmann said. 'We don't want England. If we did we would have had her long ago. We really do not want you.'

He waved his spoon airily, looking across at me as though I were a little child whom he would keep or dismiss as he pleased.

'We certainly do not want Germany,' I said.

'This morning I took a half bath. Then this afternoon I must take a knee bath and an arm bath,' volunteered the Herr Rat; 'then I do my exercises for an hour, and my work is over. A glass of wine and a couple of rolls with some sardines –'

They were handed cherry cake with whipped cream.

'What is your husband's favourite meat?' asked the Widow.

'I really do not know,' I answered.

'You really do not know? How long have you been married?'

'Three years.'

'But you cannot be in earnest! You would not have kept house as his wife for a week without knowing that fact.'

'I really never asked him; he is not at all particular about his food.'

A pause. They all looked at me, shaking their heads, their mouths full of cherry stones.

'No wonder there is a repetition in England of that dreadful state of things in Paris,' said the Widow, folding her dinner napkin. 'How can a woman expect to keep her husband if she does not know his favourite food after three years?'

'*Mahlzeit!*[2]'

'*Mahlzeit!*'

I closed the door after me.

The Baron

'Who is he?' I said. 'And why does he sit always alone, with his back to us, too?'

'Ah!' whispered the Frau Oberregierungsrat, 'he is a *Baron*.'

She looked at me very solemnly, and yet with the slightest possible contempt – a 'fancy-not-recognising-that-at-the-first-glance' expression.

'But, poor soul, he cannot help it,' I said. 'Surely that unfortunate fact ought not to debar him from the pleasures of intellectual intercourse.'

If it had not been for her fork I think she would have crossed herself.

'Surely you cannot understand. He is one of the First Barons.'

More than a little unnerved, she turned and spoke to the Frau Doktor on her left.

'My omelette is empty – *empty*,' she protested, 'and this is the third I have tried!'

I looked at the First of the Barons. He was eating salad – taking a whole lettuce leaf on his fork and absorbing it slowly, rabbit-wise – a fascinating process to watch.

Small and slight, with scanty black hair and beard and yellow-toned complexion, he invariably wore black serge clothes, a rough linen shirt, black sandals, and the largest black-rimmed spectacles that I had ever seen.

The Herr Oberlehrer, who sat opposite me, smiled benignantly.

'It must be very interesting for you, *gnädige Frau*[3], to be able to watch… of course this is a *very fine house*. There was a lady from the Spanish Court here in the summer; she had a liver. We often spoke together.'

I looked gratified and humble.

'Now, in England, in your "boarding-'ouse", one does not find the First Class, as in Germany.'

'No, indeed,' I replied, still hypnotised by the Baron, who looked like a little yellow silkworm.

'The Baron comes every year,' went on the Herr Oberlehrer, 'for his nerves. He has never spoken to any of the guests – *yet*.' A smile crossed his face. I seemed to see his visions of some splendid upheaval of that silence – a dazzling exchange of courtesies in a dim future, a splendid sacrifice of a newspaper to this Exalted One, a '*danke schön*' to be handed down to future generations.

At that moment the postman, looking like a German army officer, came in with the mail. He threw my letters into my milk pudding, and then turned to a waitress and whispered. She retired hastily. The manager of the pension came in with a little tray. A picture postcard was deposited on it, and reverently bowing his head, the manager of the pension carried it to the Baron.

Myself, I felt disappointed that there was not a salute of twenty-five guns.

At the end of the meal we were served with coffee. I noticed the Baron took three lumps of sugar, putting two in his cup and wrapping up the third in a corner of his pocket handkerchief. He was always the first to enter the dining-room and the last to leave; and in a vacant chair beside him he placed a little black leather bag.

In the afternoon, leaning from my window, I saw him pass down the street, walking tremulously and carrying the bag. Each time he passed a lamp-post he shrank a little, as though expecting it to strike him, or maybe the sense of plebeian contamination... I wondered where he was going, and why he carried the bag. Never had I seen him at the Casino or the Bath Establishment. He looked forlorn, his feet slipped in his sandals. I found myself pitying the Baron.

That evening a party of us were gathered in the salon discussing the day's *Kur*[4] with feverish animation. The Frau Oberregierungsrat sat by me knitting a shawl for her youngest of nine daughters, who was in that very interesting, frail condition... 'But it is bound to be quite satisfactory,' she said to me. 'The dear married a banker – the desire of her life.'

There must have been eight or ten of us gathered together, we who were married exchanging confidences as to the underclothing and peculiar characteristics of our husbands, the unmarried discussing the over-clothing and peculiar fascinations of Possible Ones.

'I knit them myself,' I heard the Frau Lehrer cry, 'of thick grey wool. He wears one a month, with two soft collars.'

'And then,' whispered Fräulein Lisa, 'he said to me, "Indeed you please me. I shall, perhaps, write to your mother."'

Small wonder that we were a little violently excited, a little expostulatory.

Suddenly the door opened and admitted the Baron.

Followed a complete and deathlike silence.

He came in slowly, hesitated, took up a toothpick from a dish on the top of the piano, and went out again.

When the door was closed we raised a triumphant cry! It was the first time he had ever been known to enter the salon. Who could tell what the Future held?

Days lengthened into weeks. Still we were together, and still the solitary little figure, head bowed as though under the weight of the spectacles, haunted me. He entered with the black bag, he retired with the black bag – and that was all.

At last the manager of the pension told us the Baron was leaving the next day.

'Oh,' I thought, 'surely he cannot drift into obscurity – be lost without one word! Surely he will honour the Frau Oberregierungsrat or the Frau Feldleutnantswitwe *once* before he goes.'

In the evening of that day it rained heavily. I went to the post office, and as I stood on the steps, umbrella-less, hesitating before plunging into the slushy road, a little, hesitating voice seemed to come from under my elbow.

I looked down. It was the First of the Barons with the black bag and an umbrella. Was I mad? Was I sane? He was asking me to share the latter. But I was exceedingly nice, a trifle diffident, appropriately reverential. Together we walked through the mud and slush.

Now, there is something peculiarly intimate in sharing an umbrella.

It is apt to put one on the same footing as brushing a man's coat for him – a little daring, naive.

I longed to know why he sat alone, why he carried the bag, what he did all day. But he himself volunteered some information.

'I fear,' he said, 'that my luggage will be damp. I invariably carry it with me in this bag – one requires so little – for servants are untrustworthy.'

'A wise idea,' I answered. And then: 'Why have you denied us the pleasure –'

'I sit alone that I may eat more,' said the Baron, peering into the dusk; 'my stomach requires a great deal of food. I order double portions, and eat them in peace.'

Which sounded finely Baronial.

'And what do you do all day?'

'I imbibe nourishment in my room,' he replied, in a voice that closed the conversation and almost repented of the umbrella.

When we arrived at the pension there was very nearly an open riot.

I ran halfway up the stairs, and thanked the Baron audibly from the landing.

He distinctly replied: 'Not at all!'

It was very friendly of the Herr Oberlehrer to have sent me a bouquet that evening, and the Frau Oberregierungsrat asked me for my pattern of a baby's bonnet!

Next day the Baron was gone.

Sic transit gloria German mundi.[5]

The Sister of the Baroness

'There are two new guests arriving this afternoon,' said the manager of the pension, placing a chair for me at the breakfast-table. 'I have only received the letter acquainting me with the fact this morning. The Baroness von Gall is sending her little daughter – the poor child is dumb – to make the "cure". She is to stay with us a month, and then the Baroness herself is coming.'

'Baroness von Gall,' cried the Frau Doktor, coming into the room and positively scenting the name. 'Coming here? There was a picture of her only last week in *Sport and Salon*. She is a friend of the Court: I have heard that the Kaiserin says "*du*" to her.[6] But this is delightful! I shall take my doctor's advice and spend an extra six weeks here. There is nothing like young society.'

'But the child is dumb,' ventured the manager apologetically.

'Bah! What does that matter? Afflicted children have such pretty ways.'

Each guest who came into the breakfast-room was bombarded with the wonderful news. 'The Baroness von Gall is sending her little daughter here; the Baroness herself is coming in a month's time.' Coffee and rolls took on the nature of an orgy. We positively scintillated. Anecdotes of the High Born were poured out, sweetened and sipped: we gorged on scandals of High Birth generously buttered.

'They are to have the room next to yours,' said the manager, addressing me. 'I was wondering if you would permit me to take down the portrait of the Kaiserin Elizabeth from above your bed to hang over their sofa.'

'Yes, indeed, something homelike' – the Frau Oberregierungsrat patted my hand – 'and of no possible significance to you.'

I felt a little crushed. Not at the prospect of losing that vision of diamonds and blue velvet bust, but at the tone – placing me outside the pale – branding me as a foreigner.

We dissipated the day in valid speculations. Decided it was too warm to walk in the afternoon, so lay down on our beds, mustering in great force for afternoon coffee. And a carriage drew up at the door. A tall young girl got out, leading a child by the hand. They entered the hall, were greeted and shown to their room. Ten minutes later she came down with the child to sign the visitors' book. She wore a black, closely fitting dress, touched at throat and wrists with white frilling. Her brown hair, braided, was tied with a black bow – unusually pale, with a small mole on her left cheek.

'I am the Baroness von Gall's sister,' she said, trying the pen on a piece of blotting-paper, and smiling at us deprecatingly. Even for the most jaded of us life holds its thrilling moments. Two baronesses in two months! The manager immediately left the room to find a new nib.

To my plebeian eyes that afflicted child was singularly unattractive. She had the air of having been perpetually washed with a blue bag, and hair like grey wool – dressed, too, in a pinafore so stiffly starched that she could only peer at us over the frill of it – a social barrier of a pinafore – and perhaps it was too much to expect a noble aunt to attend to the menial consideration of her niece's ears. But a dumb niece with unwashed ears struck me as a most depressing object.

They were given places at the head of the table. For a moment we all looked at one another with an eena-deena-dina-do expression.

Then the Frau Oberregierungsrat: 'I hope you are not tired after your journey.'

'No,' said the sister of the Baroness, smiling into her cup.

'I hope the dear child is not tired,' said the Frau Doktor.

'Not at all.'

'I expect, I hope you will sleep well tonight,' the Herr Oberlehrer said reverently.

'Yes.'

The poet from Munich never took his eyes off the pair. He allowed his tie to absorb most of his coffee while he gazed at them exceedingly soulfully.

Unyoking Pegasus, thought I. Death spasms of his Odes to Solitude! There were possibilities in that young woman for an inspiration, not to mention a dedication, and from that moment his suffering temperament took up its bed and walked.

They retired after the meal, leaving us to discuss them at leisure.

'There is a likeness,' mused the Frau Doktor. 'Quite. What a manner she has. Such reserve, such a tender way with the child.'

'Pity she has the child to attend to,' exclaimed the student from Bonn. He had hitherto relied upon three scars and a ribbon to produce an effect, but the sister of a Baroness demanded more than these.

Absorbing days followed. Had she been one whit less beautifully born we could not have endured the continual conversation about her, the songs in her praise, the detailed account of her movements. But she graciously suffered our worship and we were more than content.

The poet she took into her confidence. He carried her books when we went walking, he jumped the afflicted one on his knee – poetic licence, this – and one morning brought his notebook into the salon and read to us.

'The sister of the Baroness has assured me she is going into a convent,' he said. (That made the student from Bonn sit up.) 'I have written these few lines last night from my window in the sweet night air –'

'Oh, your *delicate* chest,' commented the Frau Doktor.

He fixed a stony eye on her, and she blushed.

'I have written these lines:

'Ah, will you to a convent fly,
So young, so fresh, so fair?
Spring like a doe upon the fields
And find your beauty there.'

Nine verses equally lovely commanded her to equally violent action. I am certain that had she followed his advice not even the remainder of her life in a convent would have given her time to recover her breath.

'I have presented her with a copy,' he said. 'And today we are going to look for wild flowers in the wood.'

The student from Bonn got up and left the room. I begged the poet to repeat the verses once more. At the end of the sixth verse I saw from the window the sister of the Baroness and the scarred youth disappearing through the front gate, which enabled me to thank the poet so charmingly that he offered to write me out a copy.

But we were living at too high pressure in those days. Swinging from our humble pension to the high walls of palaces, how could we help but fall? Late one afternoon the Frau Doktor came upon me in the writing-room and took me to her bosom.

'She has been telling me all about her life,' whispered the Frau Doktor. 'She came to my bedroom and offered to massage my arm. You know, I am the greatest martyr to rheumatism. And, fancy now, she has already had six proposals of marriage. Such beautiful offers that I assure you I wept – and every one of noble birth. My dear, the most beautiful was in the wood. Not that I do not think a proposal should take place in a drawing-room – it is more fitting to have four walls – but this was a private wood. He said, the young officer, she was like a young tree whose branches had never been touched by the ruthless hand of man. Such delicacy!' She sighed and turned up her eyes.

'Of course it is difficult for you English to understand when you are always exposing your legs on cricket fields, and breeding dogs in your back gardens. The pity of it! Youth should be like a wild rose. For myself I do not understand how your women ever get married at all.'

She shook her head so violently that I shook mine too, and a gloom settled round my heart. It seemed we were really in a very bad way. Did the spirit of romance spread her rose wings only over aristocratic Germany?

I went to my room, bound a pink scarf about my hair, and took a volume of Mörike's lyrics[7] into the garden. A great bush of purple lilac grew behind the summer-house. There I sat down, finding a sad significance in the delicate suggestion of half mourning. I began to write a poem myself.

They sway and languish dreamily,
And we, close-pressed, are kissing there.

It ended! 'Close-pressed' did not sound at all fascinating. Savoured of wardrobes. Did my wild rose then already trail in the dust? I chewed a leaf and hugged my knees. Then – magic moment – I heard voices from the summer-house, the sister of the Baroness and the student from Bonn.

Second-hand was better than nothing; I pricked up my ears.

'What small hands you have,' said the student from Bonn. 'They are like white lilies lying in the pool of your black dress.' This certainly sounded the real thing. Her high-born reply was what interested me. Sympathetic murmur only.

'May I hold one?' I heard two sighs – presumed they held – he had rifled those dark waters of a noble blossom.

'Look at my great fingers beside yours.'

'But they are beautifully kept,' said the sister of the Baroness shyly.

The minx! Was love then a question of manicure?

'How I should adore to kiss you,' murmured the student. 'But you know I am suffering from severe nasal catarrh, and I dare not risk giving it to you. Sixteen times last night did I count myself sneezing. And three different handkerchiefs.'

I threw Mörike into the lilac bush, and went back to the house. A great automobile snorted at the front door. In the salon great commotion. The Baroness was paying a surprise visit to her little daughter. Clad in a yellow mackintosh she stood in the middle of the room questioning the manager. And every guest the pension contained was grouped about her, even the Frau Doktor, presumably examining a timetable, as near to the august skirts as possible.

'But where is my maid?' asked the Baroness.

'There was no maid,' replied the manager, 'save for your gracious sister and daughter.'

'Sister!' she cried sharply. 'Fool, I have no sister. My child travelled with the daughter of my dressmaker.'

Tableau grandissimo![8]

Frau Fischer

Frau Fischer was the fortunate possessor of a candle factory somewhere on the banks of the Eger, and once a year she ceased from her labours to make a 'cure' in Dorschausen, arriving with a dress-basket neatly covered in a black tarpaulin and a handbag. The latter contained amongst her handkerchiefs, eau de Cologne, toothpicks, and a certain woollen muffler very comforting to the 'tummy', samples of her skill in candle-making, to be offered up as tokens of thanksgiving when her holiday time was over.

Four of the clock one July afternoon she appeared at the Pension Müller. I was sitting in the arbour and watched her bustling up the path followed by the red-bearded porter with her dress-basket in his arms and a sunflower between his teeth. The widow and her five innocent daughters stood tastefully grouped upon the steps in appropriate attitudes of welcome; and the greetings were so long and loud that I felt a sympathetic glow.

'What a journey!' cried the Frau Fischer. 'And nothing to eat in the train – nothing solid. I assure you the sides of my stomach are flapping together. But I must not spoil my appetite for dinner – just a cup of coffee in my room. Bertha,' turning to the youngest of the five, 'how changed! What a bust! Frau Hartmann, I congratulate you.'

Once again the Widow seized Frau Fischer's hands. 'Kathi, too, a splendid woman; but a little pale. Perhaps the young man from Nürnberg is here again this year. How you keep them all I don't know. Each year I come expecting to find you with an empty nest. It's surprising.'

Frau Hartmann, in an ashamed, apologetic voice: 'We are

such a happy family since my dear man died.'

'But these marriages – one must have courage; and after all, give them time, they all make the happy family bigger – thank God for that... Are there many people here just now?'

'Every room engaged.'

Followed a detailed description in the hall, murmured on the stairs, continued in six parts as they entered the large room (windows opening upon the garden) which Frau Fischer occupied each successive year. I was reading the *Miracles of Lourdes*, which a Catholic priest – fixing a gloomy eye upon my soul – had begged me to digest; but its wonders were completely routed by Frau Fischer's arrival. Not even the white roses upon the feet of the Virgin could flourish in that atmosphere.

'...*It was a simple shepherd-child who pastured her flocks upon the barren fields...*'

Voices from the room above: 'The washstand has, of course, been scrubbed over with soda.'

'...*Poverty-stricken, her limbs with tattered rags half covered...*'

'Every stick of the furniture has been sunning in the garden for three days. And the carpet we made ourselves out of old clothes. There is a piece of that beautiful flannel petticoat you left us last summer.'

'...*Deaf and dumb was the child; in fact, the population considered her half idiot...*'

'Yes, that is a new picture of the Kaiser. We have moved the thorn-crowned one of Jesus Christ out into the passage. It was not cheerful to sleep with. Dear Frau Fischer, won't you take your coffee out in the garden?'

'That is a very nice idea. But first I must remove my corsets and my boots. Ah, what a relief to wear sandals again. I am needing the "cure" very badly this year. My nerves! I am a mass of them. During the entire journey I sat with my handkerchief over my head, even while the guard collected the tickets. Exhausted!'

She came into the arbour wearing a black and white spotted dressing-gown, and a calico cap peaked with patent leather, followed by Kathi, carrying the little blue jugs of malt coffee. We were formally introduced. Frau Fischer sat down, produced a perfectly clean pocket handkerchief and polished her cup and saucer, then lifted the lid of the coffee-pot and peered in at the contents mournfully.

'Malt coffee,' she said. 'Ah, for the first few days I wonder how I can put up with it. Naturally, absent from home one must expect much discomfort and strange food. But as I used to say to my dear husband: with a clean sheet and a good cup of coffee I can find my happiness anywhere. But now, with nerves like mine, no sacrifice is too terrible for me to make. What complaint are you suffering from? You look exceedingly healthy!'

I smiled and shrugged my shoulders.

'Ah, that is so strange about you English. You do not seem to enjoy discussing the functions of the body. As well speak of a railway train and refuse to mention the engine. How can we hope to understand anybody, knowing nothing of their stomachs? In my husband's most severe illness – the poultices –'

She dipped a piece of sugar in her coffee and watched it dissolve.

'Yet a young friend of mine who travelled to England for the funeral of his brother told me that women wore bodices in public restaurants no waiter could help looking into as he handed the soup.'

'But only German waiters,' I said. 'English ones look over the top of your head.'

'There,' she cried, 'now you see your dependence on Germany. Not even an efficient waiter can you have by yourselves.'

'But I prefer them to look over your head.'

'And that proves that you must be ashamed of your bodice.'

I looked out over the garden full of wallflowers and standard rose trees growing stiffly like German bouquets, feeling I did not care one way or the other. I rather wanted to ask her if the young friend had gone to England in the capacity of waiter to attend the funeral baked meats, but decided it was not worth it. The weather was too hot to be malicious, and who could be uncharitable, victimised by the flapping sensations which Frau Fischer was enduring until six-thirty? As a gift from heaven for my forbearance, down the path towards us came the Herr Rat, angelically clad in a white silk suit. He and Frau Fischer were old friends. She drew the folds of her dressing-gown together, and made room for him on the little green bench.

'How cool you are looking,' she said; 'and if I may make the remark – what a beautiful suit!'

'Surely I wore it last summer when you were here? I brought the silk from China – smuggled it through the Russian customs by swathing it round my body. And such a quantity: two dress lengths for my sister-in-law, three suits for myself, a cloak for the housekeeper of my flat in Munich. How I perspired! Every inch of it had to be washed afterwards.'

'Surely you have had more adventures than any man in Germany. When I think of the time that you spent in Turkey with a drunken guide who was bitten by a mad dog and fell over a precipice into a field of attar of roses, I lament that you have not written a book.'

'Time – time. I am getting a few notes together. And now that you are here we shall renew our quiet little talks after supper. Yes? It is necessary and pleasant for a man to find relaxation in the company of women occasionally.'

'Indeed I realise that. Even here your life is too strenuous – you are so sought after – so admired. It was just the same with my dear husband. He was a tall, beautiful man, and sometimes in the evening he would come down into the kitchen and say: "Wife, I would like to be stupid for two minutes." Nothing rested him so much then as for me to stroke his head.'

The Herr Rat's bald pate glistening in the sunlight seemed symbolical of the sad absence of a wife.

I began to wonder as to the nature of these quiet little after-supper talks. How could one play Delilah to so shorn a Samson?

'Herr Hoffmann from Berlin arrived yesterday,' said the Herr Rat.

'That young man I refuse to converse with. He told me last year that he had stayed in France in a hotel where they did not have serviettes; what a place it must have been! In Austria even the cabmen have serviettes. Also I have heard that he discussed "free love" with Bertha as she was sweeping his room. I am not accustomed to such company. I had suspected him for a long time.'

'Young blood,' answered the Herr Rat genially. 'I have had several disputes with him – you have heard them – is it not so?' turning to me.

'A great many,' I said, smiling.

'Doubtless you, too, consider me behind the times. I make no secret of my age; I am sixty-nine; but you must have surely observed how impossible it was for him to speak at all when I raised my voice.'

I replied with the utmost conviction, and, catching Frau Fischer's eye, suddenly realised I had better go back to the house and write some letters.

It was dark and cool in my room. A chestnut tree pushed green boughs against the window. I looked down at the horsehair sofa so openly flouting the idea of curling up as immoral, pulled the red pillow on to the floor and lay down. And barely had I got comfortable when the door opened and Frau Fischer entered.

'The Herr Rat had a bathing appointment,' she said, shutting the door after her. 'May I come in? Pray do not move. You look like a little Persian kitten. Now, tell me something really interesting about your life. When I meet new people I squeeze them dry like a sponge. To begin with – you are married.'

I admit the fact.

'Then, dear child, where is your husband?'

I said he was a sea-captain on a long and perilous voyage.

'What a position to leave you in – so young and so unprotected.'

She sat down on the sofa and shook her finger at me playfully.

'Admit, now, that you keep your journeys secret from him. For what man would think of allowing a woman with such a wealth of hair to go wandering in foreign countries? Now, supposing that you lost your purse at midnight in a snowbound train in North Russia?'

'But I haven't the slightest intention –' I began.

'I don't say that you have. But when you said goodbye to your dear man I am positive that you had no intention of coming here. My dear, I am a woman of experience, and I know the world. While he is away you have a fever in your blood. Your sad heart flies for comfort to these foreign lands. At home you cannot bear the sight of that empty bed – it is like widowhood. Since the death of my dear husband I have never known an hour's peace.'

'I like empty beds,' I protested sleepily, thumping the pillow.

'That cannot be true because it is not natural. Every wife ought to feel that her place is by her husband's side – sleeping or waking. It is plain to see that the strongest tie of all does not yet bind you. Wait until a little pair of hands stretches across the water – wait until he comes into harbour and sees you with the child at your breast.'

I sat up stiffly.

'But I consider child-bearing the most ignominious of all professions,' I said.

For a moment there was silence. Then Frau Fischer reached down and caught my hand.

'So young and yet to suffer so cruelly,' she murmured. 'There is nothing that sours a woman so terribly as to be left alone without a man, especially if she is married, for then it is impossible for her to accept the attention of others – unless she is unfortunately a widow. Of course, I know that sea-captains are subject to terrible temptations, and they are as inflammable as tenor singers – that is why you must present a bright and energetic appearance, and try and make him proud of you when his ship reaches port.'

This husband that I had created for the benefit of Frau Fischer became in her hands so substantial a figure that I could no longer see myself sitting on a rock with seaweed in my hair, awaiting that phantom ship for which all women love to suppose they hunger. Rather I saw myself pushing a perambulator up the gangway, and counting up the missing buttons on my husband's uniform jacket.

'Handfuls of babies, that is what you are really in need of,' mused Frau Fischer. 'Then, as the father of a family he cannot leave you. Think of his delight and excitement when he saw you!'

The plan seemed to me something of a risk. To appear suddenly with handfuls of strange babies is not generally calculated to raise enthusiasm in the heart of the average British husband. I decided to wreck my virgin conception and send him down somewhere off Cape Horn.

Then the dinner gong sounded.

'Come up to my room afterwards,' said Frau Fischer. 'There is still much that I must ask you.'

She squeezed my hand, but I did not squeeze back.

Frau Brechenmacher Attends a Wedding

Getting ready was a terrible business. After supper Frau Brechenmacher packed four of the five babies to bed, allowing Rosa to stay with her and help to polish the buttons of Herr Brechenmacher's uniform. Then she ran over his best shirt with a hot iron, polished his boots, and put a stitch or two into his black satin necktie.

'Rosa,' she said, 'fetch my dress and hang it in front of the stove to get the creases out. Now, mind, you must look after the children and not sit up later than half-past eight, and not touch the lamp – you know what will happen if you do.'

'Yes, mamma,' said Rosa, who was nine and felt old enough to manage a thousand lamps. 'But let me stay up – the "Bub" may wake and want some milk.'

'Half-past eight!' said the Frau. 'I'll make the father tell you too.'

Rosa drew down the corners of her mouth.

'But... but...'

'Here comes the father. You go into the bedroom and fetch my blue silk handkerchief. You can wear my black shawl while I'm out – there now!'

Rosa dragged it off her mother's shoulders and wound it carefully round her own, tying the two ends in a knot at the back. After all, she reflected, if she had to go to bed at half-past eight she would keep the shawl on. Which resolution comforted her absolutely.

'Now, then, where are my clothes?' cried Herr Brechenmacher, hanging his empty letter-bag behind the door and stamping the snow out of his boots. 'Nothing ready, of course, and everybody at the wedding by this time. I heard the music as I passed. What are you doing? You're not dressed. You can't go like that.'

'Here they are – all ready for you on the table, and some warm water in the tin basin. Dip your head in. Rosa, give your father the towel. Everything ready except the trousers. I haven't had time to shorten them. You must tuck the ends into your boots until we get there.'

'*Nu*,' said the Herr, 'there isn't room to turn. I want the light. You go and dress in the passage.'

Dressing in the dark was nothing to Frau Brechenmacher. She hooked her skirt and bodice, fastened her handkerchief round her neck with a beautiful brooch that had four medals to the Virgin dangling from it, and then drew on her cloak and hood.

'Here, come and fasten this buckle,' called Herr Brechenmacher. He stood in the kitchen puffing himself out, the buttons on his blue uniform shining with an enthusiasm which nothing but official buttons could possibly possess. 'How do I look?'

'Wonderful,' replied the little Frau, straining at the waist buckle and giving him a little pull here, a little tug there. 'Rosa, come and look at your father.'

Herr Brechenmacher strode up and down the kitchen, was helped on with his coat, then waited while the Frau lit the lantern.

'Now, then – finished at last! Come along.'

'The lamp, Rosa,' warned the Frau, slamming the front door behind them.

Snow had not fallen all day; the frozen ground was slippery as an ice pond. She had not been out of the house for weeks past, and the day had so flurried her that she felt muddled and stupid – felt that Rosa had pushed her out of the house and her man was running away from her.

'Wait, wait!' she cried.

'No. I'll get my feet damp – you hurry.'

It was easier when they came into the village. There were fences to cling to, and leading from the railway station to the Gasthaus a little path of cinders had been strewn for the benefit of the wedding guests.

The Gasthaus was very festive. Lights shone out from every window, wreaths of fir twigs hung from the ledges. Branches decorated the front doors, which swung open, and in the hall the landlord voiced his superiority by bullying the waitresses, who ran about continually with glasses of beer, trays of cups and saucers, and bottles of wine.

'Up the stairs – up the stairs!' boomed the landlord. 'Leave your coats on the landing.' Herr Brechenmacher, completely overawed by this grand manner, so far forgot his rights as a husband as to beg his wife's pardon for jostling her against the banisters in his efforts to get ahead of everybody else.

Herr Brechenmacher's colleagues greeted him with acclamation as he entered the door of the Festsaal, and the Frau straightened her brooch and folded her hands, assuming the air of dignity becoming to the wife of a postman and the mother of five children. Beautiful indeed was the Festsaal. Three long tables were grouped at one end, the remainder of the floor space cleared for dancing. Oil lamps, hanging from the ceiling, shed a warm, bright light on the walls decorated with paper flowers and garlands; shed a warmer, brighter light on the red faces of the guests in their best clothes.

At the head of the centre table sat the bride and bridegroom, she in a white dress trimmed with stripes and bows of coloured ribbon, giving her the appearance of an iced cake all ready to be cut and served in neat little pieces to the bridegroom beside her, who wore a suit of white clothes much too large for him and a white silk tie that rose halfway up his collar. Grouped about them, with a fine regard for dignity and precedence, sat their parents and relations; and perched on a stool at the bride's right hand a little girl in a crumpled muslin dress with a wreath of forget-me-nots hanging over one ear. Everybody was laughing and talking, shaking hands, clinking glasses, stamping on the floor – a stench of beer and perspiration filled the air.

Frau Brechenmacher, following her man down the room after greeting the bridal party, knew that she was going to enjoy herself. She seemed to fill out and become rosy and warm as she sniffed that familiar festive smell. Somebody pulled at her skirt, and, looking down, she saw Frau Rupp, the butcher's wife, who pulled out an empty chair and begged her to sit beside her.

'Fritz will get you some beer,' she said. 'My dear, your skirt is open at the back. We could not help laughing as you walked up the room with the white tape of your petticoat showing!'

'But how frightful!' said Frau Brechenmacher, collapsing into her chair and biting her lip.

'*Na*, it's over now,' said Frau Rupp, stretching her fat hands over the table and regarding her three mourning-rings with intense enjoyment; 'but one must be careful, especially at a wedding.'

'And such a wedding as this,' cried Frau Ledermann, who sat on the other side of Frau Brechenmacher. 'Fancy Theresa bringing that child with her. It's her own child, you know, my dear, and it's going to live with them. That's what I call a sin against the Church for a free-born child to attend its own mother's wedding.'

The three women sat and stared at the bride, who remained very still, with a little vacant smile on her lips, only her eyes shifting uneasily from side to side.

'Beer they've given it, too,' whispered Frau Rupp, 'and white wine and an ice. It never did have a stomach; she ought to have left it at home.'

Frau Brechenmacher turned round and looked towards the bride's mother. She never took her eyes off her daughter, but wrinkled her brown forehead like an old monkey, and nodded now and again very solemnly. Her hands shook as she raised her beer mug, and when she had drunk she spat on the floor and savagely wiped her mouth with her sleeve. Then the music started and she followed Theresa with her eyes, looking suspiciously at each man who danced with her.

'Cheer up, old woman,' shouted her husband, digging her in the ribs; 'this isn't Theresa's funeral.' He winked at the guests, who broke into loud laughter.

'I *am* cheerful,' mumbled the old woman, and beat upon the table with her fist, keeping time to the music, proving she was not out of the festivities.

'She can't forget how wild Theresa has been,' said Frau Ledermann. 'Who could – with the child there? I heard that last Sunday evening Theresa had hysterics and said that she would not marry this man. They had to get the priest to her.'

'Where is the other one?' asked Frau Brechenmacher. 'Why didn't he marry her?'

The woman shrugged her shoulders. 'Gone – disappeared. He was a traveller, and only stayed at their house two nights. He was selling shirt buttons – I bought some myself, and they were beautiful shirt buttons – but what a pig of a fellow! I can't think what he saw in such a plain girl – but you never know. Her mother says she's been like fire ever since she was sixteen!'

Frau Brechenmacher looked down at her beer and blew a little hole in the froth.

'That's not how a wedding should be,' she said; 'it's not religion to love two men.'

'Nice time she'll have with this one,' Frau Rupp exclaimed. 'He was lodging with me last summer and I had to get rid of him. He never changed his clothes once in two months, and when I spoke to him of the smell in his room he told me he was sure it floated up from the shop. Ah, every wife has her cross. Isn't that true, my dear?'

Frau Brechenmacher saw her husband among his colleagues at the next table. He was drinking far too much, she knew – gesticulating wildly, the saliva spluttering out of his mouth as he talked.

'Yes,' she assented, 'that's true. Girls have a lot to learn.'

Wedged in between these two fat old women, the Frau had no hope of being asked to dance. She watched the couples going round and round; she forgot her five babies and her man and felt almost like a girl again. The music sounded sad and sweet. Her roughened hands clasped and unclasped themselves in the folds of her skirt. While the music went on she was afraid to look anybody in the face, and she smiled with a little nervous tremor round the mouth.

'But, my God,' Frau Rupp cried, 'they've given that child of Theresa's a piece of sausage. It's to keep her quiet. There's going to be a presentation now – your man has to speak.'

Frau Brechenmacher sat up stiffly. The music ceased, and the dancers took their places again at the tables.

Herr Brechenmacher alone remained standing – he held in his hands a big silver coffee-pot. Everybody laughed at his speech, except the Frau; everybody roared at his grimaces, and at the way he carried the coffee-pot to the bridal pair, as if it were a baby he was holding.

She lifted the lid, peeped in, then shut it down with a little scream and sat biting her lips. The bridegroom wrenched the pot away from her and drew forth a baby's bottle and two little cradles holding china dolls. As he dandled these treasures before Theresa the hot room seemed to heave and sway with laughter.

Frau Brechenmacher did not think it funny. She stared round at the laughing faces, and suddenly they all seemed strange to her. She wanted to go home and never come out again. She imagined that all these people were laughing at her, more people than there were in the room even – all laughing at her because they were so much stronger than she was.

They walked home in silence. Herr Brechenmacher strode ahead, she stumbled after him. White and forsaken lay the road from the railway station to their house – a cold rush of wind blew her hood from her face, and suddenly she remembered how they had come home together the first night. Now they had five babies and twice as much money; *but* –

'*Na*, what is it all for?' she muttered, and not until she had reached home, and prepared a little supper of meat and bread for her man did she stop asking herself that silly question.

Herr Brechenmacher broke the bread into his plate, smeared it round with his fork and chewed greedily.

'Good?' she asked, leaning her arms on the table and pillowing her breast against them.

'But fine!'

He took a piece of the crumb, wiped it round his plate edge, and held it up to her mouth. She shook her head.

'Not hungry,' she said.

'But it is one of the best pieces, and full of the fat.'

He cleared the plate; then pulled off his boots and flung them into a corner.

'Not much of a wedding,' he said, stretching out his feet and wriggling his toes in the worsted socks.

'N–no,' she replied, taking up the discarded boots and placing them on the oven to dry.

Herr Brechenmacher yawned and stretched himself, and then looked up at her, grinning.

'Remember the night that we came home? You were an innocent one, you were.'

'Get along! Such a time ago I forget.' Well she remembered.

'Such a clout on the ear as you gave me... But I soon taught you.'

'Oh, don't start talking. You've too much beer. Come to bed.'

He tilted back in his chair, chuckling with laughter.

'That's not what you said to me that night. God, the trouble you gave me!'

But the little Frau seized the candle and went into the next room. The children were all soundly sleeping. She stripped the mattress off the baby's bed to see if he was still dry, then began unfastening her blouse and skirt.

'Always the same,' she said – 'all over the world the same; but, God in heaven – but *stupid*.'

Then even the memory of the wedding faded quite. She lay down on the bed and put her arm across her face like a child who expected to be hurt as Herr Brechenmacher lurched in.

The Modern Soul

'Good evening,' said the Herr Professor, squeezing my hand; 'wonderful weather! I have just returned from a party in the wood. I have been making music for them on my trombone. You know, these pine trees provide most suitable accompaniment for a trombone! They are sighing delicacy against sustained strength, as I remarked once in a lecture on wind instruments in Frankfurt. May I be permitted to sit beside you on this bench, *gnädige Frau*?'

He sat down, tugging at a white paper package in the tail pocket of his coat.

'Cherries,' he said, nodding and smiling. 'There is nothing like cherries for producing free saliva after trombone playing, especially after Grieg's *Ich Liebe Dich*. Those sustained blasts on *liebe* make my throat as dry as a railway tunnel. Have some?' He shook the bag at me.

'I prefer watching you eat them.'

'Ah, ha!' He crossed his legs, sticking the cherry bag between his knees, to leave both hands free. 'Psychologically I understood your refusal. It is your innate feminine delicacy in preferring etherealised sensations... Or perhaps you do not care to eat the worms. All cherries contain worms. Once I made a very interesting experiment with a colleague of mine at the university. We bit into four pounds of the best cherries and did not find one specimen without a worm. But what would you? As I remarked to him afterwards – dear friend, it amounts to this: if one wishes to satisfy the desires of nature one must be strong enough to ignore the facts of nature... The conversation is not out of your depth? I have so seldom the time or opportunity to open my heart to a woman that I am apt to forget.'

I looked at him brightly.

'See what a fat one!' cried the Herr Professor. 'That is almost a mouthful in itself; it is beautiful enough to hang from a watch chain.' He chewed it up and spat the stone an incredible distance – over the garden path into the flower-bed. He was proud of the feat. I saw it. 'The quantity of fruit I have eaten on this bench,' he sighed; 'apricots, peaches and cherries. One day that garden bed will become an orchard grove, and I shall allow you to pick as much as you please, without paying me anything.'

I was grateful, without showing undue excitement.

'Which reminds me' – he hit the side of his nose with one finger – 'the manager of the pension handed me my weekly bill after dinner this evening. It is almost impossible to credit. I do not expect you to believe me – he has charged me extra for a miserable little glass of milk I drink in bed at night to prevent insomnia. Naturally, I did not pay. But the tragedy of the story is this: I cannot expect the milk to produce somnolence any longer; my peaceful attitude of mind towards it is completely destroyed. I know I shall throw myself into a fever in attempting to plumb this want of generosity in so wealthy a man as the manager of a pension. Think of me tonight' – he ground the empty bag under his heel – 'think that the worst is happening to me as your head drops asleep on your pillow.'

Two ladies came on the front steps of the pension and stood, arm in arm, looking over the garden. The one, old and scraggy, dressed almost entirely in black bead trimming and a satin reticule; the other, young and thin, in a white gown, her yellow hair tastefully garnished with mauve sweet peas.

The Professor drew in his feet and sat up sharply, pulling down his waistcoat.

'The Godowskas,' he murmured. 'Do you know them? A mother and daughter from Vienna. The mother has an internal complaint and the daughter is an actress. Fräulein Sonia is a very modern soul. I think you would find her most sympathetic. She is forced to be in attendance on her mother just now. But what a temperament! I have once described her in her autograph album as a tigress with a flower in the hair. Will you excuse me? Perhaps I can persuade them to be introduced to you.'

I said, 'I am going up to my room.' But the Professor rose and shook a playful finger at me. '*Na*,' he said, 'we are friends, and, therefore, I shall speak quite frankly to you. I think they would consider it a little "marked" if you immediately retired to the house at their approach, after sitting here alone with me in the twilight. You know this world. Yes, you know it as I do.'

I shrugged my shoulders, remarking with one eye that while the Professor had been talking the Godowskas had trailed across the lawn towards us. They confronted the Herr Professor as he stood up.

'Good evening,' quavered Frau Godowska. 'Wonderful weather! It has given me quite a touch of hay fever!' Fräulein Godowska said nothing. She swooped over a rose growing in the embryo orchard then stretched out her hand with a magnificent gesture to the Herr Professor. He presented me.

'This is my little English friend of whom I have spoken. She is the stranger in our midst. We have been eating cherries together.'

'How delightful,' sighed Frau Godowska. 'My daughter and I have often observed you through the bedroom window. Haven't we, Sonia?'

Sonia absorbed my outward and visible form with an inward and spiritual glance, then repeated the magnificent gesture for my benefit. The four of us sat on the bench, with that faint air of excitement of passengers established in a railway carriage on the qui vive for the train whistle. Frau Godowska sneezed. 'I wonder if it is hay fever,' she remarked, worrying the satin reticule for her handkerchief, 'or would it be the dew. Sonia, dear, is the dew falling?'

Fräulein Sonia raised her face to the sky, and half closed her eyes. 'No, mamma, my face is quite warm. Oh, look, Herr Professor, there are swallows in flight; they are like a little flock of Japanese thoughts – *nicht wahr?*'

'Where?' cried the Herr Professor. 'Oh yes, I see, by the kitchen chimney. But why do you say "Japanese"? Could you not compare them with equal veracity to a little flock of German thoughts in flight?' He rounded on me. 'Have you swallows in England?'

'I believe there are some at certain seasons. But doubtless they have not the same symbolical value for the English. In Germany –'

'I have never been to England,' interrupted Fräulein Sonia, 'but I have many English acquaintances. They are so cold!' She shivered.

'Fish-blooded,' snapped Frau Godowska. 'Without soul, without heart, without grace. But you cannot equal their dress materials. I spent a week in Brighton twenty years ago, and the travelling cape I bought there is not yet worn out – the one you wrap the hot-water bottle in, Sonia. My lamented husband, your father, Sonia, knew a great deal about England. But the more he knew about it the oftener he remarked to me, "England is merely an island of beef flesh swimming in a warm gulf sea of gravy." Such a brilliant way of putting things. Do you remember, Sonia?'

'I forget nothing, mamma,' answered Sonia.

Said the Herr Professor: 'That is the proof of your calling, *gnädiges Fräulein*. Now I wonder – and this is a very interesting speculation – is memory a blessing or – excuse the word – a curse?'

Frau Godowska looked into the distance, then the corners of her mouth dropped and her skin puckered. She began to shed tears.

'*Ach Gott!*[10] Gracious lady, what have I said?' exclaimed the Herr Professor.

Sonia took her mother's hand. 'Do you know,' she said, 'tonight it is stewed carrots and nut tart for supper. Suppose we go in and take our places,' her sidelong, tragic stare accusing the Professor and me the while.

I followed them across the lawn and up the steps. Frau Godowska was murmuring, 'Such a wonderful, beloved man'; with her disengaged hand Fräulein Sonia was arranging the sweet-pea 'garniture'.

A concert for the benefit of afflicted Catholic infants will take place in the salon at eight-thirty p.m. Artists: Fräulein Sonia Godowska, from Vienna; Herr Professor Windberg and his trombone; Frau Oberlehrer Weidel, and others.

This notice was tied round the neck of the melancholy stag's head in the dining-room. It graced him like a red and white dinner bib for days before the event, causing the Herr Professor to bow before it and say 'good appetite' until we sickened of his pleasantry and left the smiling to be done by the waiter, who was paid to be pleasing to the guests.

On the appointed day the married ladies sailed about the pension dressed like upholstered chairs, and the unmarried ladies like draped muslin dressing-table covers. Frau

Godowska pinned a rose in the centre of her reticule; another blossom was tucked in the mazy folds of a white antimacassar thrown across her breast. The gentlemen wore black coats, white silk ties and ferny buttonholes tickling the chin.

The floor of the salon was freshly polished, chairs and benches arranged, and a row of little flags strung across the ceiling – they flew and jigged in the draught with all the enthusiasm of family washing. It was arranged that I should sit beside Frau Godowska, and that the Herr Professor and Sonia should join us when their share of the concert was over.

'That will make you feel quite one of the performers,' said the Herr Professor genially. 'It is a great pity that the English nation is so unmusical. Never mind! Tonight you shall hear something – we have discovered a nest of talent during the rehearsals.'

'What do you intend to recite, Fräulein Sonia?'

She shook back her hair. 'I never know until the last moment. When I come on the stage I wait for one moment and then I have the sensation as though something struck me here,' – she placed her hand upon her collar brooch – 'and... words come!'

'Bend down a moment,' whispered her mother. 'Sonia, love, your skirt safety pin is showing at the back. Shall I come outside and fasten it properly for you, or will you do it yourself?'

'Oh, mamma, please don't say such things,' Sonia flushed and grew very angry. 'You know how sensitive I am to the slightest unsympathetic impression at a time like this... I would rather my skirt dropped off my body –'

'Sonia – my heart!'

A bell tinkled.

The waiter came in and opened the piano. In the heated excitement of the moment he entirely forgot what was fitting, and flicked the keys with the grimy table napkin he carried over his arm. The Frau Oberlehrer tripped on the platform followed by a very young gentleman, who blew his nose twice before he hurled his handkerchief into the bosom of the piano.

'Yes, I know you have no love for me,
And no forget-me-not.
No love, no heart, and no forget-me-not,'

sang the Frau Oberlehrer, in a voice that seemed to issue from her forgotten thimble and have nothing to do with her.

'*Ach*, how sweet, how delicate,' we cried, clapping her soothingly. She bowed as though to say, 'Yes, isn't it?' and retired, the very young gentleman dodging her train and scowling.

The piano was closed, an armchair was placed in the centre of the platform. Fräulein Sonia drifted towards it. A breathless pause. Then, presumably, the winged shaft struck her collar brooch. She implored us not to go into the woods in trained dresses, but rather as lightly draped as possible, and bed with her among the pine needles. Her loud, slightly harsh voice filled the salon. She dropped her arms over the back of the chair, moving her lean hands from the wrists. We were thrilled and silent. The Herr Professor, beside me, abnormally serious, his eyes bulging, pulled at his moustache ends. Frau Godowska adopted that peculiarly detached attitude of the proud parent. The only soul who remained untouched by her appeal was the waiter, who leant idly against the wall of the salon and cleaned his nails with the edge of a programme. He was 'off duty' and intended to show it.

'What did I say?' shouted the Herr Professor under cover of tumultuous applause, 'tem-per-ament! There you have it. She is a flame in the heart of a lily. I know I am going to play well. It is my turn now. I am inspired. Fräulein Sonia' – as that lady returned to us, pale and draped in a large shawl – 'you are my inspiration. Tonight you shall be the soul of my trombone. Wait only.'

To right and left of us people bent over and whispered admiration down Fräulein Sonia's neck. She bowed in the grand style.

'I am always successful,' she said to me. 'You see, when I act I *am*. In Vienna, in the plays of Ibsen we had so many bouquets that the cook had three in the kitchen. But it is difficult here. There is so little magic. Do you not feel it? There is none of that mysterious perfume which floats almost as a visible thing from the souls of the Viennese audiences. My spirit starves for want of that.' She leant forward, chin on hand. 'Starves,' she repeated.

The Professor appeared with his trombone, blew into it, held it up to one eye, tucked back his shirt cuffs and wallowed in the soul of Sonia Godowska. Such a sensation did he create that he was recalled to play a Bavarian dance, which he acknowledged was to be taken as a breathing exercise rather than an artistic achievement. Frau Godowska kept time to it with a fan.

Followed the very young gentleman who piped in a tenor voice that he loved somebody, 'with blood in his heart and a thousand pains'. Fräulein Sonia acted a poison scene with the assistance of her mother's pill vial and the armchair replaced by a chaise longue; a young girl scratched a lullaby on a young fiddle; and the Herr Professor performed the last sacrificial rites on the altar of the afflicted children by playing the National Anthem.

'Now I must put mamma to bed,' whispered Fräulein Sonia. 'But afterwards I must take a walk. It is imperative that I free my spirit in the open air for a moment. Would you come with me as far as the railway station and back?'

'Very well, then, knock on my door when you're ready.'

Thus the modern soul and I found ourselves together under the stars.

'What a night!' she said. 'Do you know that poem of Sappho about her hands in the stars... I am curiously sapphic. And this is so remarkable – not only am I sapphic, I find in all the works of all the greatest writers, especially in their unedited letters, some touch, some sign of myself – some resemblance, some part of myself, like a thousand reflections of my own hands in a dark mirror.'

'But what a bother,' said I.

'I do not know what you mean by "bother"; is it rather the curse of my genius...' She paused suddenly, staring at me. 'Do you know my tragedy?' she asked.

I shook my head.

'My tragedy is my mother. Living with her I live with the coffin of my unborn aspirations. You heard that about the safety pin tonight. It may seem to you a little thing, but it ruined my three first gestures. They were –'

'Impaled on a safety pin,' I suggested.

'Yes, exactly that. And when we are in Vienna I am the victim of moods, you know. I long to do wild, passionate things. And mamma says, "Please pour out my mixture first." Once I remember I flew into a rage and threw a washstand jug out of the window. Do you know what she said? "Sonia, it is not so much throwing things out of windows, if only you would –"'

‘Choose something smaller?’ said I.

‘No… “tell me about it beforehand.” Humiliating! And I do not see any possible light out of this darkness.’

‘Why don’t you join a touring company and leave your mother in Vienna?’

‘What! Leave my poor, little, sick, widowed mother in Vienna! Sooner than that I would drown myself. I love my mother as I love nobody else in the world – nobody and nothing! Do you think it is impossible to love one’s tragedy? “Out of my great sorrows I make my little songs”, that is Heine or myself.’

‘Oh, well, that’s all right,’ I said cheerfully.

‘But it is not all right!’

I suggested we should turn back. We turned.

‘Sometimes I think the solution lies in marriage,’ said Fräulein Sonia. ‘If I find a simple, peaceful man who adores me and will look after mamma – a man who would be for me a pillow – for genius cannot hope to mate – I shall marry him… You know the Herr Professor has paid me very marked attentions.’

‘Oh, Fräulein Sonia,’ I said, very pleased with myself, ‘why not marry him to your mother?’ We were passing the hairdresser’s shop at the moment. Fräulein Sonia clutched my arm.

‘You, you,’ she stammered. ‘The cruelty. I am going to faint. Mamma to marry again before I marry – the indignity. I am going to faint here and now.’

I was frightened. ‘You can’t,’ I said, shaking her. ‘Come back to the pension and faint as much as you please. But you can’t faint here. All the shops are closed. There is nobody about. Please don’t be so foolish.’

‘Here and here only!’ She indicated the exact spot and

dropped quite beautifully, lying motionless.

'Very well,' I said, 'faint away; but please hurry over it.'

She did not move. I began to walk home, but each time I looked behind me I saw the dark form of the modern soul prone before the hairdresser's window. Finally I ran, and rooted out the Herr Professor from his room. 'Fräulein Sonia has fainted,' I said crossly.

'*Du lieber Gott!*[11] Where? How?'

'Outside the hairdresser's shop in the Station Road.'

'Jesus and Maria! Has she no water with her?' – he seized his carafe – 'nobody beside her?'

'Nothing.'

'Where is my coat? No matter, I shall catch a cold on the chest. Willingly, I shall catch one... You are ready to come with me?'

'No,' I said; 'you can take the waiter.'

'But she must have a woman. I cannot be so indelicate as to attempt to loosen her stays.'

'Modern souls oughtn't to wear them,' said I. He pushed past me and clattered down the stairs.

When I came down to breakfast next morning there were two places vacant at table. Fräulein Sonia and the Herr Professor had gone off for a day's excursion in the woods.

I wondered.

At Lehmann's

Certainly Sabina did not find life slow. She was on the trot from early morning until late at night. At five o'clock she tumbled out of bed, buttoned on her clothes, wearing a long-sleeved alpaca pinafore over her black frock, and groped her way downstairs into the kitchen.

Anna, the cook, had grown so fat during the summer that she adored her bed because she did not have to wear her corsets there, but could spread as much as she liked, roll about under the great mattress, calling upon Jesus and Holy Mary and Blessed Anthony himself that her life was not fit for a pig in a cellar.

Sabina was new to her work. Pink colour still flew in her cheeks; there was a little dimple on the left side of her mouth that even when she was most serious, most absorbed, popped out and gave her away. And Anna blessed that dimple. It meant an extra half-hour in bed for her; it made Sabina light the fire, turn out the kitchen and wash endless cups and saucers that had been left over from the evening before. Hans, the scullery boy, did not come until seven. He was the son of the butcher – a mean, undersized child very much like one of his father's sausages, Sabina thought. His red face was covered with pimples, and his nails indescribably filthy. When Herr Lehmann himself told Hans to get a hairpin and clean them he said they were stained from birth because his mother had always got so inky doing the accounts – and Sabina believed him and pitied him.

Winter had come very early to Mindelbau. By the end of October the streets were banked waist-high with snow, and the greater number of the 'Cure Guests', sick unto death of cold water and herbs, had departed in nothing approaching peace. So the large salon was shut at Lehmann's and the breakfast-room was all the accommodation the café afforded. Here the floor had to be washed over, the tables rubbed, coffee-cups set out, each with its little china platter of sugar, and newspapers and magazines hung on their hooks along the walls before Herr Lehmann appeared at seven-thirty and opened business.

As a rule his wife served in the shop leading into the café, but she had chosen the quiet season to have a baby, and, a big woman at the best of times, she had grown so enormous in the process that her husband told her she looked unappetising, and had better remain upstairs and sew.

Sabina took on the extra work without any thought of extra pay. She loved to stand behind the counter, cutting up slices of Anna's marvellous chocolate-spotted confections, or doing up packets of sugar almonds in pink and blue striped bags.

'You'll get varicose veins, like me,' said Anna. 'That's what the Frau's got, too. No wonder the baby doesn't come! All her swelling's got into her legs.' And Hans was immensely interested.

During the morning business was comparatively slack. Sabina answered the shop bell, attended to a few customers who drank a liqueur to warm their stomachs before the mid-day meal, and ran upstairs now and again to ask the Frau if she wanted anything. But in the afternoon six or seven choice spirits played cards, and everybody who was anybody drank tea or coffee.

'Sabina... Sabina...'

She flew from one table to the other, counting out handfuls of small change, giving orders to Anna through the 'slide', helping the men with their heavy coats, always with that magical child air about her, that delightful sense of perpetually attending a party.

'How is the Frau Lehmann?' the women would whisper.

'She feels rather low, but as well as can be expected,' Sabina would answer, nodding confidentially.

Frau Lehmann's bad time was approaching. Anna and her friends referred to it as her 'journey to Rome', and Sabina longed to ask questions, yet, being ashamed of her ignorance, was silent, trying to puzzle it out for herself. She knew practically nothing except that the Frau had a baby inside her, which had to come out – very painful indeed. One could not have one without a husband – that she also realised. But what had the man got to do with it? So she wondered as she sat mending tea towels in the evening, head bent over her work, light shining on her brown curls. Birth – what was it? wondered Sabina. Death – such a simple thing. She had a little picture of her dead grandmother dressed in a black silk frock, tired hands clasping the crucifix that dragged between her flattened breasts, mouth curiously tight, yet almost secretly smiling. But the grandmother had been born once – that was the important fact.

As she sat there one evening, thinking, the Young Man entered the café, and called for a glass of port wine. Sabina rose slowly. The long day and the hot room made her feel a little languid, but as she poured out the wine she felt the Young Man's eyes fixed on her, looked down at him and dimpled.

'It's cold out,' she said, corking the bottle.

The Young Man ran his hands through his snow-powdered hair and laughed.

'I wouldn't call it exactly tropical,' he said, 'but you're very snug in here – look as though you've been asleep.'

Very languid felt Sabina in the hot room, and the Young Man's voice was strong and deep. She thought she had never seen anybody who looked so strong – as though he could take up the table in one hand – and his restless gaze wandering over her face and figure gave her a curious thrill deep in her body, half pleasure, half pain… She wanted to stand there, close beside him, while he drank his wine. A little silence followed. Then he took a book out of his pocket, and Sabina went back to her sewing. Sitting there in the corner, she listened to the sound of the leaves being turned and the loud ticking of the clock that hung over the gilt mirror. She wanted to look at him again – there was a something about him, in his deep voice, even in the way his clothes fitted. From the room above she heard the heavy dragging sound of Frau Lehmann's footsteps, and again the old thoughts worried Sabina. If she herself should one day look like that – feel like that! Yet it would be very sweet to have a little baby to dress and jump up and down.

'Fräulein – what's your name – what are you smiling at?' called the Young Man.

She blushed and looked up, hands quiet in her lap, looked across the empty tables and shook her head.

'Come here, and I'll show you a picture,' he commanded.

She went and stood beside him. He opened the book, and Sabina saw a coloured sketch of a naked girl sitting on the edge of a great, crumpled bed, a man's opera hat on the back of her head.

He put his hand over the body, leaving only the face exposed, then scrutinised Sabina closely.

'Well?'

'What do you mean?' she asked, knowing perfectly well.

'Why, it might be your own photograph – the face, I mean – that's as far as I can judge.'

'But the hair's done differently,' said Sabina, laughing. She threw back her head, and the laughter bubbled in her round white throat.

'It's rather a nice picture, don't you think?' he asked. But she was looking at a curious ring he wore on the hand that covered the girl's body, and only nodded.

'Ever seen anything like it before?'

'Oh, there's plenty of those funny ones in the illustrated papers.'

'How would you like to have your picture taken that way?'

'Me? I'd never let anybody see it. Besides, I haven't got a hat like that!'

'That's easily remedied.'

Again a little silence, broken by Anna throwing up the slide.

Sabina ran into the kitchen.

'Here, take this milk and egg up to the Frau,' said Anna. 'Who've you got in there?'

'Got such a funny man! I think he's a little gone here,' tapping her forehead.

Upstairs in the ugly room the Frau sat sewing, a black shawl round her shoulders, her feet encased in red woollen slippers. The girl put the milk on a table by her, then stood, polishing a spoon on her apron.

'Nothing else?'

'*Na*,' said the Frau, heaving up in her chair. 'Where's my man?'

'He's playing cards over at Snipold's. Do you want him?'

'Dear heaven, leave him alone. I'm nothing. I don't matter... And the whole day waiting here.'

Her hand shook as she wiped the rim of the glass with her fat finger.

'Shall I help you to bed?'

'You go downstairs, leave me alone. Tell Anna not to let Hans grub the sugar – give him one on the ear.'

'Ugly – ugly – ugly,' muttered Sabina, returning to the café where the Young Man stood coat-buttoned, ready for departure.

'I'll come again tomorrow,' said he. 'Don't twist your hair back so tightly; it will lose all its curl.'

'Well, you are a funny one,' she said. 'Good night.'

By the time Sabina was ready for bed Anna was snoring. She brushed out her long hair and gathered it in her hands… Perhaps it would be a pity if it lost all its curl. Then she looked down at her straight chemise, and drawing it off, sat down on the side of the bed.

'I wish,' she whispered, smiling sleepily, 'there was a great big looking-glass in this room.'

Lying down in the darkness, she hugged her little body.

'I wouldn't be the Frau for one hundred marks – not for a thousand marks. To look like that.'

And half dreaming, she imagined herself heaving up in her chair with the port wine bottle in her hand as the Young Man entered the café.

Cold and dark the next morning. Sabina woke, tired, feeling as though something heavy had been pressing under her heart all night. There was a sound of footsteps shuffling along the passage. Herr Lehmann! She must have overslept herself. Yes, he was rattling the door handle.

'One moment, one moment,' she called, dragging on her stockings.

'Bina, tell Anna to go to the Frau – but quickly. I must ride for the nurse.'

'Yes, yes!' she cried. 'Has it come?'

But he had gone, and she ran over to Anna and shook her by the shoulder.

'The Frau – the baby – Herr Lehmann for the nurse,' she stuttered.

'Name of God!' said Anna, flinging herself out of bed.

No complaints today. Importance – enthusiasm in Anna's whole bearing.

'You run downstairs and light the oven. Put on a pan of water' – speaking to an imaginary sufferer as she fastened her blouse – 'Yes, yes, I know – we must be worse before we are better – I'm coming – patience.'

It was dark all that day. Lights were turned on immediately the café opened, and business was very brisk. Anna, turned out of the Frau's room by the nurse, refused to work, and sat in a corner nursing herself, listening to sounds overhead. Hans was more sympathetic than Sabina. He also forsook work, and stood by the window, picking his nose.

'But why must I do everything?' said Sabina, washing glasses. 'I can't help the Frau; she oughtn't to take such a time about it.'

'Listen,' said Anna, 'they've moved her into the back bedroom above here, so as not to disturb the people. That was a groan – that one!'

'Two small beers,' shouted Herr Lehmann through the slide.

'One moment, one moment.'

At eight o'clock the café was deserted. Sabina sat down in the corner without her sewing. Nothing seemed to have happened to the Frau. A doctor had come – that was all.

'*Ach*,' said Sabina. 'I think no more of it. I listen no more. *Ach*, I would like to go away – I hate this talk. I will not hear it. No, it is too much.' She leant both elbows on the table – cupped her face in her hands and pouted.

But the outer door suddenly opening, she sprang to her feet and laughed. It was the Young Man again. He ordered more port, and brought no book this time.

'Don't go and sit miles away,' he grumbled. 'I want to be amused. And here, take my coat. Can't you dry it somewhere? – snowing again.'

'There's a warm place – the ladies' cloakroom,' she said. 'I'll take it in there – just by the kitchen.'

She felt better, and quite happy again.

'I'll come with you,' he said. 'I'll see where you put it.'

And that did not seem at all extraordinary. She laughed and beckoned to him.

'In here,' she cried. 'Feel how warm. I'll put more wood on that oven. It doesn't matter, they're all busy upstairs.'

She knelt down on the floor, and thrust the wood into the oven, laughing at her own wicked extravagance.

The Frau was forgotten, the stupid day was forgotten. Here was someone beside her laughing, too. They were together in the little warm room stealing Herr Lehmann's wood. It seemed the most exciting adventure in the world. She wanted to go on laughing – or burst out crying – or – or – catch hold of the Young Man.

'What a fire,' she shrieked, stretching out her hands.

'Here's a hand; pull up,' said the Young Man. 'There, now, you'll catch it tomorrow.'

They stood opposite to each other, hands still clinging. And again that strange tremor thrilled Sabina.

'Look here,' he said roughly, 'are you a child, or are you playing at being one?'

'I – I –' Laughter ceased. She looked up at him once, then down at the floor, and began breathing like a frightened little animal.

He pulled her closer still and kissed her mouth.

'*Na*, what are you doing?' she whispered.

He let go her hands, he placed his on her breasts, and the room seemed to swim round Sabina. Suddenly, from the room above, a frightful, tearing shriek.

She wrenched herself away, tightened herself, drew herself up.

'Who did that – who made that noise?'

In the silence the thin wailing of a baby.

'*Achk!*' shrieked Sabina, rushing from the room.

The Luft Bad

I think it must be the umbrellas which make us look ridiculous.

When I was admitted into the enclosure for the first time, and saw my fellow-bathers walking about very nearly 'in their nakeds', it struck me that the umbrellas gave a distinctly 'Little Black Sambo' touch.

Ridiculous dignity in holding over yourself a green cotton thing with a red parakeet handle when you are dressed in nothing larger than a handkerchief.

There are no trees in the 'Luft Bad'. It boasts a collection of plain, wooden cells, a bath shelter, two swings and two odd clubs – one, presumably the lost property of Hercules or the German army, and the other to be used with safety in the cradle.

And there in all weathers we take the air – walking, or sitting in little companies, talking over each other's ailments and measurements and ills that flesh is heir to.

A high wooden wall compasses us all about; above it the pine trees look down a little superciliously, nudging each other in a way that is peculiarly trying to a debutante. Over the wall, on the right side, is the men's section. We hear them chopping down trees and sawing through planks, dashing heavy weights to the ground, and singing part-songs. Yes, they take it far more seriously.

On the first day I was conscious of my legs, and went back into my cell three times to look at my watch, but when a woman with whom I had played chess for three weeks cut me dead, I took heart and joined a circle.

We lay curled on the ground while a Hungarian lady of

immense proportions told us what a beautiful tomb she had bought for her second husband.

'A vault it is,' she said, 'with nice black railings. And so large that I can go down there and walk about. Both their photographs are there, with two very handsome wreaths sent me by my first husband's brother. There is an enlargement of a family group photograph, too, and an illuminated address presented to my first husband on his marriage. I am often there; it makes such a pleasant excursion for a fine Saturday afternoon.'

She suddenly lay down flat on her back, took in six long breaths, and sat up again.

'The death agony was dreadful,' she said brightly; 'of the second, I mean. The "first" was run into by a furniture wagon, and had fifty marks stolen out of a new waistcoat pocket, but the "second" was dying for sixty-seven hours. I never ceased crying once – not even to put the children to bed.'

A young Russian, with a 'bang' curl on her forehead, turned to me.

'Can you do the "Salome" dance?' she asked. 'I can.'

'How delightful,' I said.

'Shall I do it now? Would you like to see me?'

She sprang to her feet, executed a series of amazing contortions for the next ten minutes, and then paused, panting, twisting her long hair.

'Isn't that nice?' she said. 'And now I am perspiring so splendidly. I shall go and take a bath.'

Opposite to me was the brownest woman I have ever seen, lying on her back, her arms clasped over her head.

'How long have you been here today?' she was asked.

'Oh, I spend the day here now,' she answered. 'I am making my own "cure", and living entirely on raw vegetables and nuts, and each day I feel my spirit is stronger and purer. After all, what can you expect? The majority of us are walking about with pig corpuscles and oxen fragments in our brain. The wonder is the world is as good as it is. Now I live on the simple, provided food' – she pointed to a little bag beside her – 'a lettuce, a carrot, a potato, and some nuts are ample, rational nourishment. I wash them under the tap and eat them raw, just as they come from the harmless earth – fresh and uncontaminated.'

'Do you take nothing else all day?' I cried.

'Water. And perhaps a banana if I wake in the night.' She turned round and leant on one elbow. 'You overeat yourself dreadfully,' she said; 'shamelessly! How can you expect the Flame of the Spirit to burn brightly under layers of superfluous flesh?'

I wished she would not stare at me, and thought of going to look at my watch again when a little girl wearing a string of coral beads joined us.

'The poor Frau Hauptmann cannot join us today,' she said; 'she has come out in spots all over on account of her nerves. She was very excited yesterday after having written two postcards.'

'A delicate woman,' volunteered the Hungarian, 'but pleasant. Fancy, she has a separate plate for each of her front teeth! But she has no right to let her daughters wear such short sailor suits. They sit about on benches, crossing their legs in a most shameless manner. What are you going to do this afternoon, Fräulein Anna?'

'Oh,' said the Coral Necklace, 'the Herr Oberleutnant has asked me to go with him to Landsdorf. He must buy some eggs there to take home to his mother. He saves a penny on eight eggs by knowing the right peasants to bargain with.'

‘Are you an American?’ said the Vegetable Lady, turning to me.

‘No.’

‘Then you are an Englishwoman?’

‘Well, hardly –’

‘You must be one of the two; you cannot help it. I have seen you walking alone several times. You wear your –’

I got up and climbed onto the swing. The air was sweet and cool, rushing past my body. Above, white clouds trailed delicately through the blue sky. From the pine forest streamed a wild perfume, the branches swayed together, rhythmically, sonorously. I felt so light and free and happy – so childish! I wanted to poke my tongue out at the circle on the grass, who, drawing close together, were whispering meaningly.

‘Perhaps you do not know,’ cried a voice from one of the cells, ‘to swing is very upsetting for the stomach? A friend of mine could keep nothing down for three weeks after exciting herself so.’

I went to the bath shelter and was hosed.

As I dressed, someone tapped on the wall.

‘Do you know,’ said a voice, ‘there is a man who *lives* in the Luft Bad next door? He buries himself up to the armpits in mud and refuses to believe in the Trinity.’

The umbrellas are the saving grace of the Luft Bad. Now when I go, I take my husband’s ‘storm’ gamp and sit in a corner, hiding behind it.

Not that I am in the least ashamed of my legs.

A Birthday

Andreas Binzer woke slowly. He turned over on the narrow bed and stretched himself – yawned – opening his mouth as widely as possible and bringing his teeth together afterwards with a sharp 'click'. The sound of that click fascinated him; he repeated it quickly several times, with a snapping movement of the jaws. What teeth! he thought. Sound as a bell, every man jack of them. Never had one out, never had one stopped. That comes of no tomfoolery in eating, and a good regular brushing night and morning. He raised himself on his left elbow and waved his right arm over the side of the bed to feel for the chair where he put his watch and chain overnight. No chair was there – of course, he'd forgotten, there wasn't a chair in this wretched spare room. Had to put the confounded thing under his pillow. 'Half-past eight, Sunday, breakfast at nine – time for the bath' – his brain ticked to the watch. He sprang out of bed and went over to the window. The venetian blind was broken, hung fan-shaped over the upper pane… 'That blind must be mended. I'll get the office boy to drop in and fix it on his way home tomorrow – he's a good hand at blinds. Give him twopence and he'll do it as well as a carpenter… Anna could do it herself if she was all right. So would I, for the matter of that, but I don't like to trust myself on rickety stepladders.' He looked up at the sky: it shone, strangely white, unflecked with cloud; he looked down at the row of garden strips and backyards. The fence of these gardens was built along the edge of a gully, spanned by an iron suspension bridge, and the people had a wretched habit of throwing their empty tins over the fence into the gully. Just like them, of course! Andreas started counting the tins, and decided, viciously, to write a letter to the papers about it and sign it – sign it in full.

The servant girl came out of their back door into the yard, carrying his boots. She threw one down on the ground, thrust her hand into the other, and stared at it, sucking in her cheeks. Suddenly she bent forward, spat on the toecap, and started polishing with a brush rooted out of her apron pocket… 'Slut of a girl! Heaven knows what infectious disease may be breeding now in that boot. Anna must get rid of that girl – even if she has to do without one for a bit – as soon as she's up and about again. The way she chucked one boot down and then spat upon the other! She didn't care whose boots she'd got hold of. *She* had no false notions of the respect due to the master of the house.' He turned away from the window and switched his bath towel from the washstand rail, sick at heart. 'I'm too sensitive for a man – that's what's the matter with me. Have been from the beginning, and will be to the end.'

There was a gentle knock at the door and his mother came in. She closed the door after her and leant against it. Andreas noticed that her cap was crooked, and a long tail of hair hung over her shoulder. He went forward and kissed her.

'Good morning, mother; how's Anna?'

The old woman spoke quickly, clasping and unclasping her hands.

'Andreas, please go to Doctor Erb as soon as you are dressed.'

'Why,' he said, 'is she bad?'

Frau Binzer nodded, and Andreas, watching her, saw her face suddenly change; a fine network of wrinkles seemed to pull over it from under the skin surface.

'Sit down on the bed a moment,' he said. 'Been up all night?'

'Yes. No, I won't sit down, I must go back to her. Anna has

been in pain all night. She wouldn't have you disturbed before because she said you looked so run down yesterday. You told her you had caught a cold and been very worried.'

Straight away Andreas felt that he was being accused.

'Well, she made me tell her, worried it out of me; you know the way she does.'

Again Frau Binzer nodded.

'Oh yes, I know. She says, is your cold better, and there's a warm undervest for you in the left-hand corner of the big drawer.'

Quite automatically Andreas cleared his throat twice.

'Yes,' he answered. 'Tell her my throat certainly feels looser. I suppose I'd better not disturb her?'

'No, and besides, *time*, Andreas.'

'I'll be ready in five minutes.'

They went into the passage. As Frau Binzer opened the door of the front bedroom, a long wail came from the room.

That shocked and terrified Andreas. He dashed into the bathroom, turned on both taps as far as they would go, cleaned his teeth and pared his nails while the water was running.

'Frightful business, frightful business,' he heard himself whispering. 'And I can't understand it. It isn't as though it were her first – it's her third. Old Schäfer told me, yesterday, his wife simply "dropped" her fourth. Anna ought to have had a qualified nurse. Mother gives way to her. Mother spoils her. I wonder what she meant by saying I'd worried Anna yesterday. Nice remark to make to a husband at a time like this. Unstrung, I suppose – and my sensitiveness again.'

When he went into the kitchen for his boots, the servant girl was bent over the stove, cooking breakfast. 'Breathing into that, now, I suppose,' thought Andreas, and was very short with the servant girl. She did not notice. She was full of terrified joy and importance in the goings-on upstairs. She felt she was learning the secrets of life with every breath she drew. Had laid the table that morning saying, 'Boy,' as she put down the first dish, 'Girl,' as she placed the second – it had worked out with the salt spoon to 'Boy'. 'For two pins I'd tell the master that, to comfort him, like,' she decided. But the master gave her no opening.

'Put an extra cup and saucer on the table,' he said; 'the doctor may want some coffee.'

'The doctor, sir?' The servant girl whipped a spoon out of a pan, and spilt two drops of grease on the stove. 'Shall I fry something extra?' But the master had gone, slamming the door after him. He walked down the street – there was nobody about at all – dead and alive this place on a Sunday morning. As he crossed the suspension bridge a strong stench of fennel and decayed refuse streamed from the gully, and again Andreas began concocting a letter. He turned into the main road. The shutters were still up before the shops. Scraps of newspaper, hay, and fruit skins strewed the pavement; the gutters were choked with the leavings of Saturday night. Two dogs sprawled in the middle of the road, scuffling and biting. Only the public house at the corner was open; a young barman slopped water over the doorstep.

Fastidiously, his lips curling, Andreas picked his way through the water. 'Extraordinary how I am noticing things this morning. It's partly the effect of Sunday. I loathe a Sunday when Anna's tied by the leg and the children are away. On Sunday a man has the right to expect his family. Everything here's filthy, the whole place might be down with the plague, and will be, too, if this street's not swept away. I'd like to have a hand on the government ropes.' He braced his shoulders. 'Now for this doctor.'

‘Doctor Erb is at breakfast,’ the maid informed him. She showed him into the waiting-room, a dark and musty place, with some ferns under a glass case by the window. ‘He says he won’t be a minute, please, sir, and there is a paper on the table.’

‘Unhealthy hole,’ thought Binzer, walking over to the window and drumming his fingers on the glass fern-shade. ‘At breakfast, is he? That’s the mistake I made: turning out early on an empty stomach.’

A milk cart rattled down the street, the driver standing at the back, cracking a whip; he wore an immense geranium flower stuck in the lapel of his coat. Firm as a rock he stood, bending back a little in the swaying cart. Andreas craned his neck to watch him all the way down the road, even after he had gone, listening for the sharp sound of those rattling cans.

‘H’m, not much wrong with him,’ he reflected. ‘Wouldn’t mind a taste of that life myself. Up early, work all over by eleven o’clock, nothing to do but loaf about all day until milking time.’ Which he knew was an exaggeration, but he wanted to pity himself.

The maid opened the door, and stood aside for Doctor Erb. Andreas wheeled round; the two men shook hands.

‘Well, Binzer,’ said the doctor jovially, brushing some crumbs from a pearl-coloured waistcoat, ‘son and heir becoming importunate?’

Up went Binzer’s spirits with a bound. Son and heir, by Jove! He was glad to have to deal with a man again. And a sane fellow this, who came across this sort of thing every day of the week.

‘That’s about the measure of it, doctor,’ he answered, smiling and picking up his hat. ‘Mother dragged me out of bed this morning with imperative orders to bring you along.’

‘Gig will be round in a minute. Drive back with me, won’t

you? Extraordinary, sultry day; you're as red as a beetroot already.'

Andreas affected to laugh. The doctor had one annoying habit – imagined he had the right to poke fun at everybody simply because he was a doctor. 'The man's riddled with conceit, like all these professionals,' Andreas decided.

'What sort of night did Frau Binzer have?' asked the doctor. 'Ah, here's the gig. Tell me on the way up. Sit as near the middle as you can, will you, Binzer? Your weight tilts it over a bit one side – that's the worst of you successful businessmen.'

'Two stone heavier than I, if he's a pound,' thought Andreas. 'The man may be all right in his profession – but heaven preserve me.'

'Off you go, my beauty.' Doctor Erb flicked the little brown mare. 'Did your wife get any sleep last night?'

'No; I don't think she did,' answered Andreas shortly. 'To tell you the truth, I'm not satisfied that she hasn't a nurse.'

'Oh, your mother's worth a dozen nurses,' cried the doctor, with immense gusto. 'To tell you the truth, I'm not keen on nurses – too raw – raw as rump-steak. They wrestle for a baby as though they were wrestling with Death for the body of Patroclus...[12] Ever seen that picture by an English artist. Leighton? Wonderful thing – full of sinew!'

'There he goes again,' thought Andreas, 'airing off his knowledge to make a fool of me.'

'Now your mother – she's firm – she's capable. Does what she's told with a fund of sympathy. Look at these shops we're passing – they're festering sores. How on earth this government can tolerate –'

'They're not so bad – sound enough – only want a coat of paint.'

The doctor whistled a little tune and flicked the mare again.

'Well, I hope the young shaver won't give his mother too much trouble,' he said. 'Here we are.'

A skinny little boy, who had been sliding up and down the back seat of the gig, sprang out and held the horse's head. Andreas went straight into the dining-room and left the servant girl to take the doctor upstairs. He sat down, poured out some coffee, and bit through half a roll before helping himself to fish. Then he noticed there was no hotplate for the fish – the whole house was at sixes and sevens. He rang the bell, but the servant girl came in with a tray holding a bowl of soup and a hotplate.

'I've been keeping them on the stove,' she simpered.

'Ah, thanks, that's very kind of you.' As he swallowed the soup his heart warmed to this fool of a girl.

'Oh, it's a good thing Doctor Erb has come,' volunteered the servant girl, who was bursting for want of sympathy.

'H'm, h'm,' said Andreas.

She waited a moment, expectantly, rolling her eyes, then in full loathing of menkind went back to the kitchen and vowed herself to sterility.

Andreas cleared the soup bowl, and cleared the fish. As he ate, the room slowly darkened. A faint wind sprang up and beat the tree branches against the window. The dining-room looked over the breakwater of the harbour, and the sea swung heavily in rolling waves. Wind crept round the house, moaning drearily.

'We're in for a storm. That means I'm boxed up here all day. Well, there's one blessing; it'll clear the air.' He heard the servant girl rushing importantly round the house, slamming windows. Then he caught a glimpse of her in the garden, unpegging tea towels from the line across the lawn. She was a worker, there was no doubt about that. He took up a book, and wheeled his armchair over to the window. But it was useless. Too dark to read; he didn't believe in straining his eyes, and gas at ten o'clock in the morning seemed absurd. So he slipped down in the chair, leant his elbows on the padded arms and gave himself up, for once, to idle dreaming. 'A boy? Yes, it was bound to be a boy this time…' 'What's your family, Binzer?' 'Oh, I've two girls and a boy!' A very nice little number. Of course he was the last man to have a favourite child, but a man needed a son. 'I'm working up the business for my son! Binzer & Son! It would mean living very tight for the next ten years, cutting expenses as fine as possible; and then –'

A tremendous gust of wind sprang upon the house, seized it, shook it, dropped, only to grip the more tightly. The waves swelled up along the breakwater and were whipped with broken foam. Over the white sky flew tattered streamers of grey cloud.

Andreas felt quite relieved to hear Doctor Erb coming down the stairs; he got up and lit the gas.

'Mind if I smoke in here?' asked Doctor Erb, lighting a cigarette before Andreas had time to answer. 'You don't smoke, do you? No time to indulge in pernicious little habits!'

'How is she now?' asked Andreas, loathing the man.

'Oh, well as can be expected, poor little soul. She begged me to come down and have a look at you. Said she knew you were worrying.' With laughing eyes the doctor looked at the breakfast-table. 'Managed to peck a bit, I see, eh?'

'Hoo-wih!' shouted the wind, shaking the window sashes.

'Pity – this weather,' said Doctor Erb.

'Yes, it gets on Anna's nerves, and it's just nerve she wants.'

'Eh, what's that?' retorted the doctor. 'Nerve! Man alive!

She's got twice the nerve of you and me rolled into one. Nerve! she's nothing but nerve. A woman who works as she does about the house and has three children in four years thrown in with the dusting, so to speak!'

He pitched his half-smoked cigarette into the fireplace and frowned at the window.

'Now *he's* accusing me,' thought Andreas. 'That's the second time this morning – first mother and now this man taking advantage of my sensitiveness.' He could not trust himself to speak, and rang the bell for the servant girl.

'Clear away the breakfast things,' he ordered. 'I can't have them messing about on the table till dinner!'

'Don't be hard on the girl,' coaxed Doctor Erb. 'She's got twice the work to do today.'

At that Binzer's anger blazed out.

'I'll trouble you, doctor, not to interfere between me and my servants!' And he felt a fool at the same moment for not saying 'servant'.

Doctor Erb was not perturbed. He shook his head, thrust his hands into his pockets, and began balancing himself on toe and heel.

'You're jagged by the weather,' he said wryly, 'nothing else. A great pity – this storm. You know climate has an immense effect upon birth. A fine day perks a woman – gives her heart for her business. Good weather is as necessary to a confinement as it is to a washing-day. Not bad – that last remark of mine – for a professional fossil, eh?'

Andreas made no reply.

'Well, I'll be getting back to my patient. Why don't you take a walk, and clear your head? That's the idea for you.'

'No,' he answered, 'I won't do that; it's too rough.'

He went back to his chair by the window. While the servant

girl cleared away he pretended to read… then his dreams! It seemed years since he had had the time to himself to dream like that – he never had a breathing space. Saddled with work all day, and couldn't shake it off in the evening like other men. Besides, Anna was interested – they talked of practically nothing else together. Excellent mother she'd make for a boy; she had a grip of things.

Church-bells started ringing through the windy air, now sounding as though from very far away, then again as though all the churches in the town had been suddenly transplanted into their street. They stirred something in him, those bells, something vague and tender. Just about that time Anna would call him from the hall. 'Andreas, come and have your coat brushed. I'm ready.' Then off they would go, she hanging on his arm, and looking up at him. She certainly was a little thing. He remembered once saying when they were engaged, 'Just as high as my heart,' and she had jumped onto a stool and pulled his head down, laughing. A kid in those days, younger than her children in nature, brighter, more 'go' and 'spirit' in her. The way she'd run down the road to meet him after business! And the way she laughed when they were looking for a house. By Jove! that laugh of hers! At the memory he grinned, then grew suddenly grave. Marriage certainly changed a woman far more than it did a man. Talk about sobering down. She had lost all her go in two months! Well, once this boy business was over she'd get stronger. He began to plan a little trip for them. He'd take her away and they'd loaf about together somewhere. After all, dash it, they were young still. She'd got into a groove; he'd have to force her out of it, that's all.

He got up and went into the drawing-room, carefully shut the door, and took Anna's photograph from the top of the piano. She wore a white dress with a big bow of some soft stuff under the chin, and stood, a little stiffly, holding a sheaf of artificial poppies and corn in her hands. Delicate she looked even then; her masses of hair gave her that look. She seemed to droop under the heavy braids of it, and yet she was smiling. Andreas caught his breath sharply. She was his wife – that girl. Posh! it had only been taken four years ago. He held it close to him, bent forward and kissed it. Then rubbed the glass with the back of his hand. At that moment, fainter than he had heard in the passage, more terrifying, Andreas heard again that wailing cry. The wind caught it up in mocking echo, blew it over the house-tops, down the street, far away from him. He flung out his arms, 'I'm so damnably helpless,' he said, and then, to the picture, 'Perhaps it's not as bad as it sounds; perhaps it is just my sensitiveness.' In the half-light of the drawing-room the smile seemed to deepen in Anna's portrait, and to become secret, even cruel. 'No,' he reflected, 'that smile is not at all her happiest expression – it was a mistake to let her have it taken smiling like that. She doesn't look like my wife – like the mother of my son.' Yes, that was it, she did not look like the mother of a son who was going to be a partner in the firm. The picture got on his nerves; he held it in different lights, looked at it from a distance, sideways, spent – it seemed to Andreas afterwards – a whole lifetime trying to fit it in. The more he played with it the deeper grew his dislike of it. Thrice he carried it over to the fireplace and decided to chuck it behind the Japanese umbrella in the grate; then he thought it absurd to waste an expensive frame. There was no good in beating about the bush. Anna looked like a stranger – abnormal, a freak – it might be a picture taken just before or after death.

Suddenly he realised that the wind had dropped, that the whole house was still, terribly still. Cold and pale, with a disgusting feeling that spiders were creeping up his spine and across his face, he stood in the centre of the drawing-room, hearing Doctor Erb's footsteps descending the stairs.

He saw Doctor Erb come into the room; the room seemed to change into a great glass bowl that spun round, and Doctor Erb seemed to swim through this glass bowl towards him, like a goldfish in a pearl-coloured waistcoat.

'My beloved wife has passed away!' He wanted to shout it out before the doctor spoke.

'Well, she's hooked a boy this time!' said Doctor Erb. Andreas staggered forward.

'Look out. Keep on your pins,' said Doctor Erb, catching Dinzer's arm, and murmuring, as he felt it, 'Flabby as butter.'

A glow spread all over Andreas. He was exultant.

'Well, by God! Nobody can accuse *me* of not knowing what suffering is,' he said.

The Child-Who-Was-Tired

She was just beginning to walk along a little white road with tall black trees on either side, a little road that led to nowhere, and where nobody walked at all, when a hand gripped her shoulder, shook her, slapped her ear.

'Oh, oh, don't stop me,' cried the Child-Who-Was-Tired. 'Let me go.'

'Get up, you good-for-nothing brat,' said a voice; 'get up and light the oven or I'll shake every bone out of your body.'

With an immense effort she opened her eyes, and saw the Frau standing by, the baby bundled under one arm. The three other children who shared the same bed with the Child-Who-Was-Tired, accustomed to brawls, slept on peacefully. In a corner of the room the Man was fastening his braces.

'What do you mean by sleeping like this the whole night through – like a sack of potatoes? You've let the baby wet his bed twice.'

She did not answer, but tied her petticoat string, and buttoned on her plaid frock with cold, shaking fingers.

'There, that's enough. Take the baby into the kitchen with you, and heat that cold coffee on the spirit-lamp for the master, and give him the loaf of black bread out of the table drawer. Don't guzzle it yourself or I'll know.'

The Frau staggered across the room, flung herself onto her bed, drawing the pink bolster round her shoulders.

It was almost dark in the kitchen. She laid the baby on the wooden settle, covering him with a shawl, then poured the coffee from the earthenware jug into the saucepan, and set it on the spirit-lamp to boil.

'I'm sleepy,' nodded the Child-Who-Was-Tired, kneeling

on the floor and splitting the damp pine logs into little chips. 'That's why I'm not awake.'

The oven took a long time to light. Perhaps it was cold, like herself, and sleepy… Perhaps it had been dreaming of a little white road with black trees on either side, a little road that led to nowhere.

Then the door was pulled violently open and the Man strode in.

'Here, what are you doing, sitting on the floor?' he shouted. 'Give me my coffee. I've got to be off. Ugh! You haven't even washed over the table.'

She sprang to her feet, poured his coffee into an enamel cup, and gave him bread and a knife, then, taking a wash rag from the sink, smeared over the black linoleumed table.

'Swine of a day – swine's life,' mumbled the Man, sitting by the table and staring out of the window at the bruised sky, which seemed to bulge heavily over the dull land. He stuffed his mouth with bread and then swilled it down with the coffee.

The Child drew a pail of water, turned up her sleeves, frowning the while at her arms, as if to scold them for being so thin, so much like little stunted twigs, and began to mop over the floor.

'Stop sousing about the water while I'm here,' grumbled the Man. 'Stop the baby snivelling; it's been going on like that all night.'

The Child gathered the baby into her lap and sat rocking him.

'Ts – ts – ts,' she said. 'He's cutting his eye-teeth, that's what makes him cry so. *And* dribble – I never seen a baby dribble like this one.' She wiped his mouth and nose with a corner of her skirt. 'Some babies get their teeth without you knowing it,' she went on, 'and some take on this way all the time. I once heard of a baby that died, and they found all its teeth in its stomach.'

The Man got up, unhooked his cloak from the back of the door, and flung it round him.

'There's another coming,' said he.

'What – a tooth!' exclaimed the Child, startled for the first time that morning out of her dreadful heaviness, and thrusting her finger into the baby's mouth.

'No,' he said grimly, 'another baby. Now, get on with your work; it's time the others got up for school.' She stood a moment quite silently, hearing his heavy steps on the stone passage, then the gravel walk, and finally the slam of the front gate.

'Another baby! Hasn't she finished having them *yet*?' thought the Child. 'Two babies getting eye-teeth – two babies to get up for in the night – two babies to carry about and wash their little piggy clothes!' She looked with horror at the one in her arms, who, seeming to understand the contemptuous loathing of her tired glance, doubled his fists, stiffened his body, and began violently screaming.

'Ts – ts – ts.' She laid him on the settle and went back to her floor-washing. He never ceased crying for a moment, but she got quite used to it and kept time with her broom. Oh, how tired she was! Oh, the heavy broom handle and the burning spot just at the back of her neck that ached so, and a funny little fluttering feeling just at the back of her waistband, as though something were going to break.

The clock struck six. She set the pan of milk in the oven, and went into the next room to wake and dress the three children. Anton and Hans lay together in attitudes of mutual amity which certainly never existed out of their sleeping hours. Lena was curled up, her knees under her chin, only a straight, standing-up pigtail of hair showing above the bolster.

'Get up,' cried the Child, speaking in a voice of immense authority, pulling off the bedclothes and giving the boys sundry pokes and digs. 'I've been calling you this last half-hour. It's late, and I'll tell on you if you don't get dressed this minute.'

Anton awoke sufficiently to turn over and kick Hans on a tender part, whereupon Hans pulled Lena's pigtail until she shrieked for her mother.

'Oh, do be quiet,' whispered the Child. 'Oh, do get up and dress. You know what will happen. There – I'll help you.'

But the warning came too late. The Frau got out of bed, walked in a determined fashion into the kitchen, returning with a bundle of twigs in her hand fastened together with a strong cord. One by one she laid the children across her knee and severely beat them, expending a final burst of energy on the Child-Who-Was-Tired, then returned to bed, with a comfortable sense of her maternal duties in good working order for the day. Very subdued, the three allowed themselves to be dressed and washed by the Child, who even laced the boys' boots, having found through experience that if left to themselves they hopped about for at least five minutes to find a comfortable ledge for their foot, and then spat on their hands and broke the bootlaces.

While she gave them their breakfast they became uproarious, and the baby would not cease crying. When she filled the tin kettle with milk, tied on the rubber teat, and, first moistening it herself, tried with little coaxing words to make him drink, he threw the bottle onto the floor and trembled all over.

'Eye-teeth!' shouted Hans, hitting Anton over the head with his empty cup; 'he's getting the evil-eye teeth, I should say.'

'Smarty!' retorted Lena, poking out her tongue at him, and then, when he promptly did the same, crying at the top of her voice, 'Mother, Hans is making faces at me!'

'That's right,' said Hans; 'go on howling, and when you're in bed tonight I'll wait till you're asleep, and then I'll creep over and take a little tiny piece of your arm and twist and twist it until –' He leant over the table making the most horrible faces at Lena, not noticing that Anton was standing behind his chair until the little boy bent over and spat on his brother's shaven head.

'Oh, weh! oh, weh!'

The Child-Who-Was-Tired pushed and pulled them apart, muffled them into their coats, and drove them out of the house.

'Hurry, hurry! the second bell's rung,' she urged, knowing perfectly well she was telling a story, and rather exulting in the fact. She washed up the breakfast things, then went down to the cellar to look out the potatoes and beetroot.

Such a funny, cold place the coal-cellar! With potatoes banked on one corner, beetroot in an old candle box, two tubs of sauerkraut, and a twisted mass of dahlia roots – that looked as real as though they were fighting one another, thought the Child.

She gathered the potatoes into her skirt, choosing big ones with few eyes because they were easier to peel, and bending over the dull heap in the silent cellar, she began to nod.

'Here, you, what are you doing down there?' cried the Frau, from the top of the stairs. 'The baby's fallen off the settle, and got a bump as big as an egg over his eye. Come up here, and I'll teach you!'

'It wasn't me – it wasn't me!' screamed the Child, beaten from one side of the hall to the other, so that the potatoes and beetroot rolled out of her skirt.

The Frau seemed to be as big as a giant, and there was a certain heaviness in all her movements that was terrifying to anyone so small.

'Sit in the corner, and peel and wash the vegetables, and keep the baby quiet while I do the washing.'

Whimpering she obeyed, but as to keeping the baby quiet, that was impossible. His face was hot, little beads of sweat stood all over his head, and he stiffened his body and cried. She held him on her knees, with a pan of cold water beside her for the cleaned vegetables and the 'ducks' bucket' for the peelings.

'Ts – ts – ts!' she crooned, scraping and boring; 'there's going to be another soon, and you can't both keep on crying. Why don't you go to sleep, baby? I would, if I were you. I'll tell you a dream. Once upon a time there was a little white road –'

She shook back her head, a great lump ached in her throat and then the tears ran down her face onto the vegetables.

'That's no good,' said the Child, shaking them away. 'Just stop crying until I've finished this, baby, and I'll walk you up and down.'

But by that time she had to peg out the washing for the Frau. A wind had sprung up. Standing on tiptoe in the yard, she almost felt she would be blown away. There was a bad smell coming from the ducks' coop, which was half full of manure water, but away in the meadow she saw the grass blowing like little green hairs. And she remembered having heard of a child who had once played for a whole day in just such a meadow with real sausages and beer for her dinner – and not a little bit of tiredness. Who had told her that story? She could not remember, and yet it was so plain.

The wet clothes flapped in her face as she pegged them; danced and jigged on the line, bulged out and twisted. She walked back to the house with lagging steps, looking longingly at the grass in the meadow.

'What must I do now, please?' she said.

'Make the beds and hang the baby's mattress out of the window, then get the wagon and take him for a little walk along the road. In front of the house, mind – where I can see you. Don't stand there, gaping! Then come in when I call you and help me cut up the salad.'

When she had made the beds the Child stood and looked at them. Gently she stroked the pillow with her hand, and then, just for one moment, let her head rest there. Again the smarting lump in her throat, the stupid tears that fell and kept on falling as she dressed the baby and dragged the little wagon up and down the road.

A man passed, driving a bullock wagon. He wore a long, queer feather in his hat, and whistled as he passed. Two girls with bundles on their shoulders came walking out of the village – one wore a red handkerchief about her head and one a blue. They were laughing and holding each other by the hand. Then the sun pushed by a heavy fold of grey cloud and spread a warm yellow light over everything.

'Perhaps,' thought the Child-Who-Was-Tired, 'if I walked far enough up this road I might come to a little white one, with tall black trees on either side – a little road –'

'Salad, salad!' cried the Frau's voice from the house.

Soon the children came home from school, dinner was eaten, the Man took the Frau's share of pudding as well as his own, and the three children seemed to smear themselves all over with whatever they ate. Then more dish-washing and more cleaning and baby-minding. So the afternoon dragged coldly through.

Old Frau Grathwohl came in with a fresh piece of pig's flesh for the Frau, and the Child listened to them gossiping together.

'Frau Manda went on her "journey to Rome" last night, and brought back a daughter. How are you feeling?'

'I was sick twice this morning,' said the Frau. 'My insides are all twisted up with having children too quickly.'

'I see you've got a new help,' commented old Mother Grathwohl.

'Oh, dear Lord,' – the Frau lowered her voice – 'don't you know her? She's the free-born one – daughter of the waitress at the railway station. They found her mother trying to squeeze her head in the wash-hand jug, and the child's half silly.'

'Ts – ts – ts!' whispered the 'free-born' one to the baby.

As the day drew in the Child-Who-Was-Tired did not know how to fight her sleepiness any longer. She was afraid to sit down or stand still. As she sat at supper the Man and the Frau seemed to swell to an immense size as she watched them, and then become smaller than dolls, with little voices that seemed to come from outside the window. Looking at the baby, it suddenly had two heads, and then no head. Even his crying made her feel worse. When she thought of the nearness of bedtime she shook all over with excited joy. But as eight o'clock approached there was the sound of wheels on the road, and presently in came a party of friends to spend the evening.

Then it was:

'Put on the coffee.'

'Bring me the sugar tin.'

'Carry the chairs out of the bedroom.'

'Set the table.'

And, finally, the Frau sent her into the next room to keep the baby quiet.

There was a little piece of candle burning in the enamel bracket. As she walked up and down she saw her great big shadow on the wall like a grown-up person with a grown-up baby. Whatever would it look like when she carried two babies so!

'Ts – ts – ts!' Once upon a time she was walking along a little white road, with oh! such great big black trees on either side.'

'Here you!' called the Frau's voice, 'bring me my new jacket from behind the door.' And as she took it into the warm room one of the women said, 'She looks like an owl. Such children are seldom right in their heads.'

'Why don't you keep that baby quiet?' said the Man, who had just drunk enough beer to make him feel very brave and master of his house.

'If you don't keep that baby quiet you'll know why later on.'

They burst out laughing as she stumbled back into the bedroom.

'I don't believe Holy Mary could keep him quiet,' she murmured. 'Did Jesus cry like this when He was little? If I was not so tired perhaps I could do it; but the baby just knows that I want to go to sleep. And there is going to be another one.'

She flung the baby on the bed, and stood looking at him with terror. From the next room there came the jingle of glasses and the warm sound of laughter.

And she suddenly had a beautiful marvellous idea.

She laughed for the first time that day, and clapped her hands.

‘Ts – ts – ts!’ she said, ‘lie there, silly one; you *will* go to sleep. You’ll not cry any more or wake up in the night. Funny, little, ugly baby.’

He opened his eyes, and shrieked loudly at the sight of the Child-Who-Was-Tired. From the next room she heard the Frau call out to her.

‘One moment – he is almost asleep,’ she cried.

And then gently, smiling, on tiptoe, she brought the pink bolster from the Frau’s bed and covered the baby’s face with it, pressed with all her might as he struggled, ‘like a duck with its head off, wriggling,’ she thought.

She heaved a long sigh, then fell back onto the floor, and was walking along a little white road with tall black trees on either side, a little road that led to nowhere, and where nobody walked at all – nobody at all.

The Advanced Lady

'Do you think we might ask her to come with us,' said Fräulein Elsa, retying her pink sash ribbon before my mirror. 'You know, although she is so intellectual, I cannot help feeling convinced that she has some secret sorrow. And Lisa told me this morning, as she was turning out my room, that she remains hours and hours by herself, writing; in fact Lisa says she is writing a book! I suppose that is why she never cares to mingle with us, and has so little time for her husband and the child.'

'Well, *you* ask her,' said I. 'I have never spoken to the lady.'

Elsa blushed faintly. 'I have only spoken to her once,' she confessed. 'I took her a bunch of wild flowers, to her room, and she came to the door in a white gown, with her hair loose. Never shall I forget that moment. She just took the flowers, and I heard her – because the door was not quite properly shut – I heard her, as I walked down the passage, saying "Purity, fragrance, the fragrance of purity and the purity of fragrance!" It was wonderful!'

At that moment Frau Kellermann knocked at the door.

'Are you ready?' she said, coming into the room and nodding to us very genially. 'The gentlemen are waiting on the steps, and I have asked the Advanced Lady to come with us.'

'*Na*, how extraordinary!' cried Elsa. 'But this moment the *gnädige Frau* and I were debating whether –'

'Yes, I met her coming out of her room and she said she was charmed with the idea. Like all of us, she has never been to Schlingen. She is downstairs now, talking to Herr Erchardt. I think we shall have a delightful afternoon.'

'Is Fritzi waiting too?' asked Elsa.

'Of course he is, dear child – as impatient as a hungry man listening for the dinner-bell. Run along!'

Elsa ran, and Frau Kellermann smiled at me significantly. In the past she and I had seldom spoken to each other, owing to the fact that her 'one remaining joy' – her charming little Karl – had never succeeded in kindling into flame those sparks of maternity which are supposed to glow in great numbers upon the altar of every respectable female heart; but, in view of a premeditated journey together, we became delightfully cordial.

'For us,' she said, 'there will be a double joy. We shall be able to watch the happiness of these two dear children, Elsa and Fritz. They only received the letters of blessing from their parents yesterday morning. It is a very strange thing, but whenever I am in the company of newly engaged couples I blossom. Newly engaged couples, mothers with first babies, and normal deathbeds have precisely the same effect on me. Shall we join the others?'

I was longing to ask her why normal deathbeds should cause anyone to burst into flower, and said, 'Yes, do let us.'

We were greeted by the little party of 'cure guests' on the pension steps, with those cries of joy and excitement which herald so pleasantly the mildest German excursion. Herr Erchardt and I had not met before that day, so, in accordance with strict pension custom, we asked each other how long we had slept during the night, had we dreamed agreeably, what time we had got up, was the coffee fresh when we had appeared at breakfast, and how had we passed the morning. Having toiled up these stairs of almost national politeness we landed, triumphant and smiling, and paused to recover breath.

'And now,' said Herr Erchardt, 'I have a pleasure in store

for you. The Frau Professor is going to be one of us for the afternoon. Yes,' nodding graciously to the Advanced Lady. 'Allow me to introduce you to each other.'

We bowed very formally, and looked each other over with that eye which is known as 'eagle' but is far more the property of the female than that most unoffending of birds. 'I think you are English?' she said. I acknowledged the fact. 'I am reading a great many English books just now – rather, I am studying them.'

'*Nu*,' cried Herr Erchardt. 'Fancy that! What a bond already! I have made up my mind to know Shakespeare in his mother tongue before I die, but that you, Frau Professor, should be already immersed in those wells of English thought!'

'From what I have read,' she said, 'I do not think they are very deep wells.'

He nodded sympathetically.

'No,' he answered, 'so I have heard... But do not let us embitter our excursion for our little English friend. We will speak of this another time.'

'*Nu*, are we ready?' cried Fritz, who stood, supporting Elsa's elbow in his hand, at the foot of the steps. It was immediately discovered that Karl was lost.

'Ka-rl, Karl-chen!' we cried. No response.

'But he was here one moment ago,' said Herr Langen, a tired, pale youth, who was recovering from a nervous breakdown due to much philosophy and little nourishment. 'He was sitting here, picking out the works of his watch with a hairpin!'

Frau Kellermann rounded on him. 'Do you mean to say, my dear Herr Langen, you did not stop the child!'

'No,' said Herr Langen; 'I've tried stopping him before now.'

'*Da*, that child has such energy; never is his brain at peace. If he is not doing one thing, he is doing another!'

'Perhaps he has started on the dining-room clock now,' suggested Herr Langen, abominably hopeful.

The Advanced Lady suggested that we should go without him. 'I never take my little daughter for walks,' she said. 'I have accustomed her to sitting quietly in my bedroom from the time I go out until I return!'

'There he is – there he is,' piped Elsa, and Karl was observed slithering down a chestnut tree, very much the worse for twigs.

'I've been listening to what you said about me, mumma,' he confessed, while Frau Kellermann brushed him down. 'It was not true about the watch. I was only looking at it, and the little girl never stays in the bedroom. She told me herself she always goes down to the kitchen, and –'

'*Da*, that's enough!' said Frau Kellermann.

We marched en masse along the station road. It was a very warm afternoon, and continuous parties of 'cure guests', who were giving their digestions a quiet airing in pension gardens, called after us, asked if we were going for a walk, and cried '*Herr Gott*[13] – happy journey' with immense ill-concealed relish when we mentioned Schlingen.

'But that is eight kilometres,' shouted one old man with a white beard, who leant against a fence, fanning himself with a yellow handkerchief.

'Seven and a half,' answered Herr Erchardt shortly.

'Eight,' bellowed the sage.

'Seven and a half!'

'Eight!'

'The man is mad,' said Herr Erchardt.

'Well, please let him be mad in peace,' said I, putting

my hands over my ears.

'Such ignorance must not be allowed to go uncontradicted,' said he, and turning his back on us, too exhausted to cry out any longer, he held up seven and a half fingers.

'Eight!' thundered the greybeard, with pristine freshness.

We felt very sobered, and did not recover until we reached a white signpost which entreated us to leave the road and walk through the field path – without trampling down more of the grass than was necessary. Being interpreted, it meant 'single file', which was distressing for Elsa and Fritz. Karl, like a happy child, gambolled ahead, and cut down as many flowers as possible with the stick of his mother's parasol – followed the three others – then myself – and the lovers in the rear. And above the conversation of the advance party I had the privilege of hearing these delicious whispers.

Fritz: 'Do you love me?' Elsa: '*Nu* – yes.' Fritz passionately: 'But how much?' To which Elsa never replied – except with, 'How much do *you* love *me*?'

Fritz escaped that truly Christian trap by saying, 'I asked you first.'

It grew so confusing that I slipped in front of Frau Kellermann – and walked in the peaceful knowledge that she was blossoming and I was under no obligation to inform even my nearest and dearest as to the precise capacity of my affections. 'What right have they to ask each other such questions the day after letters of blessing have been received?' I reflected. 'What right have they even to question each other? Love which becomes engaged and married is a purely affirmative affair – they are usurping the privileges of their betters and wisers!'

The edges of the field frilled over into an immense pine forest – very pleasant and cool it looked. Another signpost begged us to keep to the broad path for Schlingen and deposit waste paper and fruit peelings in wire receptacles attached to the benches for the purpose. We sat down on the first bench, and Karl with great curiosity explored the wire receptacle.

'I love woods,' said the Advanced Lady, smiling pitifully into the air. 'In a wood my hair already seems to stir and remember something of its savage origin.'

'But speaking literally,' said Frau Kellermann, after an appreciative pause, 'there is really nothing better than the air of pine trees for the scalp.'

'Oh, Frau Kellermann, please don't break the spell,' said Elsa.

The Advanced Lady looked at her very sympathetically. 'Have you, too, found the magic heart of Nature?' she said.

That was Herr Langen's cue. 'Nature has no heart,' said he, very bitterly and readily, as people do who are over-philosophised and underfed. 'She creates that she may destroy. She eats that she may spew up and she spews up that she may eat. That is why we, who are forced to eke out an existence at her trampling feet, consider the world mad, and realise the deadly vulgarity of production.'

'Young man,' interrupted Herr Erchardt, 'you have never lived and you have never suffered!'

'Oh, excuse me – how can you know?'

'*I* know because you have told me, and there's an end of it. Come back to this bench in ten years' time and repeat those words to me,' said Frau Kellermann, with an eye upon Fritz, who was engaged in counting Elsa's fingers with passionate fervour – 'and bring with you your young wife, Herr Langen, and watch, perhaps, your little child playing with –' She turned towards Karl, who had rooted an old illustrated paper out of the receptacle and was spelling over an advertisement for the enlargement of Beautiful Breasts.

The sentence remained unfinished. We decided to move on. As we plunged more deeply into the wood our spirits rose – reaching a point where they burst into song – on the part of the three men – '*O Welt, wie bist du wunderbar!*'[14] – the lower part of which was piercingly sustained by Herr Langen, who attempted quite unsuccessfully to infuse satire into it in accordance with his – 'world outlook'. They strode ahead and left us to trail after them – hot and happy.

'Now is the opportunity,' said Frau Kellermann. 'Dear Frau Professor, do tell us a little about your book.'

'*Ach*, how did you know I was writing one?' she cried playfully.

'Elsa, here, had it from Lisa. And never before have I personally known a woman who was writing a book. How do you manage to find enough to write down?'

'That is never the trouble,' said the Advanced Lady – she took Elsa's arm and leant on it gently. 'The trouble is to know where to stop. My brain has been a hive for years, and about three months ago the pent-up waters burst over my soul, and since then I am writing all day until late into the night, still ever finding fresh inspirations and thoughts which beat impatient wings about my heart.'

'Is it a novel?' asked Elsa shyly.

'Of course it is a novel,' said I.

'How can you be so positive?' said Frau Kellermann, eyeing me severely.

'Because nothing but a novel could produce an effect like that.'

'*Ach*, don't quarrel,' said the Advanced Lady sweetly. 'Yes, it is a novel – upon the Modern Woman. For this seems to me the woman's hour. It is mysterious and almost prophetic, it is the symbol of the true advanced woman: not one of those violent creatures who deny their sex and smother their frail wings under… under –'

'The English tailor-made?' from Frau Kellermann.

'I was not going to put it like that. Rather, under the lying garb of false masculinity!'

'Such a subtle distinction!' I murmured.

'Whom then,' asked Fräulein Elsa, looking adoringly at the Advanced Lady – 'whom then do you consider the true woman?'

'She is the incarnation of comprehending Love!'

'But my dear Frau Professor,' protested Frau Kellermann, 'you must remember that one has so few opportunities for exhibiting Love within the family circle nowadays. One's husband is at business all day, and naturally desires to sleep when he returns home – one's children are out of the lap and in at the university before one can lavish anything at all upon them!'

'But Love is not a question of lavishing,' said the Advanced Lady. 'It is the lamp carried in the bosom touching with serene rays all the heights and depths of –'

'Darkest Africa,' I murmured flippantly.

She did not hear.

'The mistake we have made in the past – as a sex,' said she, 'is in not realising that our gifts of giving are for the whole world – we are the glad sacrifice of ourselves!'

'Oh!' cried Elsa rapturously, and almost bursting into gifts as she breathed – 'how I know that! You know ever since Fritz and I have been engaged, I share the desire to give to everybody, to share everything!'

'How extremely dangerous,' said I.

'It is only the beauty of danger, or the danger of beauty,' said the Advanced Lady – 'and there you have the ideal of my book – that woman is nothing but a gift.'

I smiled at her very sweetly. 'Do you know,' I said, 'I, too, would like to write a book, on the advisability of caring for daughters, and taking them for airings and keeping them out of kitchens!'

I think the masculine element must have felt these angry vibrations: they ceased from singing, and together we climbed out of the wood, to see Schlingen below us, tucked in a circle of hills, the white houses shining in the sunlight, 'for all the world like eggs in a bird's nest', as Herr Erchardt declared. We descended upon Schlingen and demanded sour milk with fresh cream and bread at the Inn of the Golden Stag, a most friendly place, with tables in a rose garden where hens and chickens ran riot – even flopping upon the disused tables and pecking at the red checks on the cloths. We broke the bread into the bowls, added the cream, and stirred it round with flat wooden spoons, the landlord and his wife standing by.

'Splendid weather!' said Herr Erchardt, waving his spoon at the landlord, who shrugged his shoulders.

'What! you don't call it splendid!'

'As you please,' said the landlord, obviously scorning us.

'Such a beautiful walk,' said Fräulein Elsa, making a free gift of her most charming smile to the landlady.

'I never walk,' said the landlady; 'when I go to Mindelbau my man drives me – I've more important things to do with my legs than walk them through the dust!'

'I like these people,' confessed Herr Langen to me. 'I like them very, very much. I think I shall take a room here for the whole summer.'

'Why?'

'Oh, because they live close to the earth, and therefore despise it.'

He pushed away his bowl of sour milk and lit a cigarette. We ate, solidly and seriously, until those seven and a half kilometres to Mindelbau stretched before us like an eternity. Even Karl's activity became so full-fed that he lay on the ground and removed his leather waistbelt. Elsa suddenly leant over to Fritz and whispered, who on hearing her to the end and asking her if she loved him, got up and made a little speech.

'We – we wish to celebrate our betrothal by – by – asking you all to drive back with us in the landlord's cart – if – it will hold us!'

'Oh, what a beautiful, noble idea!' said Frau Kellermann, heaving a sigh of relief that audibly burst two hooks.

'It is my little gift,' said Elsa to the Advanced Lady, who by virtue of three portions almost wept tears of gratitude.

Squeezed into the peasant cart and driven by the landlord, who showed his contempt for Mother Earth by spitting savagely every now and again, we jolted home again, and the nearer we came to Mindelbau the more we loved it and one another.

'We must have many excursions like this,' said Herr Erchardt to me, 'for one surely gets to know a person in the simple surroundings of the open air – one *shares* the same joys – one feels friendship. What is it your Shakespeare says? One moment, I have it. "The friends thou hast, and their adoption tried – grapple them to thy soul with hoops of steel!"[15]'

'But,' said I, feeling very friendly towards him, 'the bother about my soul is that it refuses to grapple anybody at all – and I am sure that the dead weight of a friend whose adoption it had tried would kill it immediately. Never yet has it shown the slightest sign of a hoop!'

He bumped against my knees and excused himself and the cart.

'My dear little lady, you must not take the quotation literally. Naturally, one is not physically conscious of the hoops; but hoops there are in the soul of him or her who loves his fellow-men… Take this afternoon, for instance. How did we start out? As strangers you might almost say, and yet – all of us – how have we come home?'

'In a cart,' said the only remaining joy, who sat upon his mother's lap and felt sick.

We skirted the field that we had passed through, going round by the cemetery. Herr Langen leant over the edge of the seat and greeted the graves. He was sitting next to the Advanced Lady – inside the shelter of her shoulder. I heard her murmur: 'You look like a little boy with your hair blowing about in the wind.' Herr Langen, slightly less bitter, watched the last graves disappear. And I heard her murmur: 'Why are you so sad? I too am very sad sometimes – but – you look young enough for me to dare to say this – I – too – know of much joy!'

'What do you know?' said he.

I leant over and touched the Advanced Lady's hand. 'Hasn't it been a nice afternoon?' I said questioningly. 'But you know, that theory of yours about women and Love – it's as old as the hills – oh, older!'

From the road a sudden shout of triumph. Yes, there he was again – white beard, silk handkerchief and undaunted enthusiasm.

'What did I say? Eight kilometres – it is!'

'Seven and a half!' shrieked Herr Erchardt.

'Why, then, do you return in carts? Eight kilometres it must be.'

Herr Erchardt made a cup of his hands and stood up in the jolting cart while Frau Kellermann clung to his knees. 'Seven and a half!'

'Ignorance must not go uncontradicted!' I said to the Advanced Lady.

The Swing of the Pendulum

The landlady knocked at the door.

'Come in,' said Viola.

'There is a letter for you,' said the landlady, 'a special letter' – she held the green envelope in a corner of her dingy apron.

'Thanks.' Viola, kneeling on the floor, poking at the little dusty stove, stretched out her hand. 'Any answer?'

'No; the messenger has gone.'

'Oh, all right!' She did not look the landlady in the face; she was ashamed of not having paid her rent, and wondered grimly, without any hope, if the woman would begin to bluster again.

'About this money owing to me –' said the landlady.

'Oh, the Lord – off she goes!' thought Viola, turning her back on the woman and making a grimace at the stove.

'It's settle – or it's go!' The landlady raised her voice; she began to bawl. 'I'm a landlady, I am, and a respectable woman, I'll have you know. I'll have no lice in my house, sneaking their way into the furniture and eating up everything. It's cash – or out you go before twelve o'clock tomorrow.'

Viola felt rather than saw the woman's gesture. She shot out her arm in a stupid helpless way, as though a dirty pigeon had suddenly flown at her face. 'Filthy old beast! Ugh! And the smell of her – like stale cheese and damp washing.'

'Very well!' she answered shortly; 'it's cash down or I leave tomorrow. All right: don't shout.'

It was extraordinary – always before this woman came near her she trembled in her shoes – even the sound of those flat feet stumping up the stairs made her feel sick, but once they were face to face she felt immensely calm and indifferent, and could not understand why she even worried about money, nor why she sneaked out of the house on tiptoe, not even daring to shut the door after her in case the landlady should hear and shout something terrible, nor why she spent nights pacing up and down her room – drawing up sharply before the mirror and saying to a tragic reflection: 'Money, money, money!' When she was alone her poverty was like a huge dream-mountain on which her feet were fast rooted – aching with the ache of the size of the thing – but if it came to definite action, with no time for imaginings, her dream-mountain dwindled into a beastly 'hold-your-nose' affair, to be passed as quickly as possible, with anger and a strong sense of superiority.

The landlady bounced out of the room, banging the door, so that it shook and rattled as though it had listened to the conversation and fully sympathised with the old hag.

Squatting on her heels, Viola opened the letter. It was from Casimir:

I shall be with you at three o'clock this afternoon – and must be off again this evening. All news when we meet. I hope you are happier than I.

– Casimir

'Huh! how kind!' she sneered; 'how condescending. Too good of you, really!' She sprang to her feet, crumbling the letter in her hands. 'And how are you to know that I shall stick here awaiting your pleasure until three o'clock this afternoon?' But she knew she would; her rage was only half sincere. She longed to see Casimir, for she was confident that this time she would make him understand the situation… 'For, as it is, it's intolerable – intolerable!' she muttered.

It was ten o'clock in the morning of a grey day curiously lit by pale flashes of sunshine. Searched by these flashes her room looked tumbled and grimed. She pulled down the window-blinds – but they gave a persistent, whitish glare which was just as bad. The only thing of life in the room was a jar of hyacinths given her by the landlady's daughter: it stood on the table exuding a sickly perfume from its plump petals; there were even rich buds unfolding, and the leaves shone like oil.

Viola went over to the washstand, poured some water into the enamel basin, and sponged her face and neck. She dipped her face into the water, opened her eyes, and shook her head from side to side – it was exhilarating. She did it three times. 'I suppose I could drown myself if I stayed under long enough,' she thought. 'I wonder how long it takes to become unconscious?… Often read of women drowning in a bucket. I wonder if any air enters by the ears – if the basin would have to be as deep as a bucket?' She experimented – gripped the washstand with both hands and slowly sank her head into the water, when again there was a knock on the door. Not the landlady this time – it must be Casimir. With her face and hair dripping, with her petticoat bodice unbuttoned, she ran and opened it.

A strange man stood against the lintel – seeing her, he opened his eyes very wide and smiled delightfully. 'Excuse me – does Fräulein Schäfer live here?'

'No; never heard of her.' His smile was so infectious, she wanted to smile too – and the water had made her feel so fresh and rosy.

The strange man appeared overwhelmed with astonishment. 'She doesn't?' he cried. 'She is out, you mean!'

'No, she's not living here,' answered Viola.

'But – pardon – one moment.' He moved from the door

lintel, standing squarely in front of her. He unbuttoned his greatcoat and drew a slip of paper from the breast pocket, smoothing it in his gloved fingers before handing it to her.

'Yes, that's the address, right enough, but there must be a mistake in the number. So many lodging-houses in this street, you know, and so big.'

Drops of water fell from her hair onto the paper. She burst out laughing. 'Oh, *how* dreadful I must look – one moment!' She ran back to the washstand and caught up a towel. The door was still open… After all, there was nothing more to be said. Why on earth had she asked him to wait a moment? She folded the towel round her shoulders, and returned to the door, suddenly grave. 'I'm sorry; I know no such name,' in a sharp voice.

Said the strange man: 'Sorry, too. Have you been living here long?'

'Er – yes – a long time.' She began to close the door slowly.

'Well – good morning, thanks so much. Hope I haven't been a bother.'

'Good morning.'

She heard him walk down the passage and then pause – lighting a cigarette. Yes – a faint scent of delicious cigarette smoke penetrated her room. She sniffed at it, smiling again. Well, that had been a fascinating interlude! He looked so amazingly happy: his heavy clothes and big buttoned gloves; his beautifully brushed hair… and that smile… 'Jolly' was the word – just a well-fed boy with the world for his playground. People like that did one good – one felt 'made over' at the sight of them. *Sane* they were – so sane and solid. You could depend on them never having one mad impulse from the day they were born until the day they died. And Life was in league with them – jumped them on her knee – quite rightly, too. At that moment she noticed Casimir's letter, crumpled up on the floor – the smile faded. Staring at the letter she began braiding her hair – a dull feeling of rage crept through her – she seemed to be braiding it into her brain, and binding it, tightly, above her head… Of course that had been the mistake all along. What had? Oh, Casimir's frightful seriousness. If she had been happy when they first met she never would have looked at him – but they had been like two patients in the same hospital ward – each finding comfort in the sickness of the other – sweet foundation for a love episode! Misfortune had knocked their heads together: they had looked at each other, stunned with the conflict, and sympathised… 'I wish I could step outside the whole affair and just judge it – then I'd find a way out. I certainly was in love with Casimir… Oh, be sincere for once.' She flopped down on the bed and hid her face in the pillow. 'I was not in love. I wanted somebody to look after me – and keep me until my work began to sell – and he kept bothers with other men away. And what would have happened if he hadn't come along? I would have spent my wretched little pittance, and then – Yes, that was what decided me, thinking about that "then". He was the only solution. And I believed in him then. I thought his work had only to be recognised once, and he'd roll in wealth. I thought perhaps we might be poor for a month – but he said, if only he could have me, the stimulus… Funny, if it wasn't so damned tragic! Exactly the contrary has happened – he hasn't had a thing published for months – neither have I – but then I didn't expect to. Yes, the truth is, I'm hard and bitter, and I have neither faith nor love for unsuccessful men. I always end by despising them as I despise Casimir. I suppose it's the savage pride of the female who likes to think the man to whom she has given herself must be a very great chief indeed. But to stew in this disgusting house while Casimir scours the land in the hope of finding one editorial open door – it's humiliating. It's changed my whole nature. I wasn't born for poverty – I only flower among really jolly people, and people who never are worried.'

The figure of the strange man rose before her – would not be dismissed. 'That was the man for me, after all is said and done – a man without a care – who'd give me everything I want and with whom I'd always feel that sense of life and of being in touch with the world. I never wanted to fight – it was thrust on me. Really, there's a fount of happiness in me, that is drying up, little by little, in this hateful existence. I'll be dead if this goes on – and' – she stirred in the bed and flung out her arms – 'I want passion, and love, and adventure – I yearn for them. Why should I stay here and rot? – I am rotting!' she cried, comforting herself with the sound of her breaking voice. 'But if I tell Casimir all this when he comes this afternoon, and he says, "Go" – as he certainly will – that's another thing I loathe about him – he's under my thumb – what should I do then – where should I go to?' There was nowhere. 'I don't want to work – or carve out my own path. I want ease and any amount of nursing in the lap of luxury. There is only one thing I'm fitted for, and that is to be a great courtesan.' But she did not know how to go about it. She was frightened to go into the streets – she heard of such awful things happening to those women – men with diseases – or men who didn't pay – besides, the idea of a strange man every night – no, that was out of the question. 'If I'd the clothes I would go to a really good hotel and find some wealthy man… like the strange man this morning. He would be ideal. Oh, if I only had his address – I am sure I would fascinate him. I'd keep him laughing all day – I'd make him give me unlimited money…' At the thought she grew warm and soft. She began to dream of a wonderful house, and of presses full of clothes, and of perfumes. She saw herself stepping into carriages – looking at the strange man with a mysterious, voluptuous glance – she practised the glance, lying on the bed – and never another worry, just drugged with happiness. That was the life for her. Well, the thing to do was to let Casimir go on his wild-goose chase that evening, and while he was away – What! Also – please to remember – there was the rent to be paid before twelve next morning, and she hadn't the money for a square meal. At the thought of food she felt a sharp twinge in her stomach, a sensation as though there were a hand in her stomach, squeezing it dry. She was terribly hungry – all Casimir's fault – and that man had lived on the fat of the land ever since he was born. He looked as though he could order a magnificent dinner. Oh, why hadn't she played her cards better? – he'd been sent by Providence – and she'd snubbed him. 'If I had that time over again, I'd be safe by now.' And instead of the ordinary man who had spoken with her at the door her mind created a brilliant, laughing image, who would treat her like a queen… 'There's only one thing I could not stand – that he should be coarse or vulgar. Well, he wasn't – he was obviously a man of the world, and the way he apologised… I have enough faith in my own power and beauty to know I could make a man treat me just as I wanted to be treated.'… It floated into her dreams – that sweet scent of cigarette smoke. And then she remembered that she had heard nobody go down the stone stairs. Was it possible that the strange man was still there?… The thought was too absurd – Life didn't play tricks like that – and yet – she was quite conscious of his nearness. Very quietly she got up, unhooked from the back of the door a long white gown, buttoned it on – smiling slyly. She did not know what was going to happen.

She only thought: 'Oh, what fun!' and that they were playing a delicious game – this strange man and she. Very gently she turned the door handle, screwing up her face and biting her lip as the lock snapped back. Of course, there he was – leaning against the banister rail. He wheeled round as she slipped into the passage.

'*Da*,' she muttered, folding her gown tightly around her, 'I must go downstairs and fetch some wood. Brr! the cold!'

'There isn't any wood,' volunteered the strange man. She gave a little cry of astonishment, and then tossed her head.

'You again,' she said scornfully, conscious the while of his merry eye, and the fresh, strong smell of his healthy body.

'The landlady shouted out there was no wood left. I just saw her go out to buy some.'

'Story – story!' she longed to cry.

He came quite close to her, stood over her and whispered: 'Aren't you going to ask me to finish my cigarette in your room?'

She nodded. 'You may if you want to!'

In that moment together in the passage a miracle had happened. Her room was quite changed – it was full of sweet light and the scent of hyacinth flowers. Even the furniture appeared different – exciting. Quick as a flash she remembered childish parties when they had played charades, and one side had left the room and come in again to act a word – just what she was doing now. The strange man went over to the stove and sat down in her armchair. She did not want him to talk or come near her – it was enough to see him in the room, so secure and happy. How hungry she had been for the nearness of someone like that – who knew nothing at all about her – and made no demands – but just lived. Viola ran over to the table and put her arms round the jar of hyacinths.

'Beautiful! Beautiful!' she cried – burying her head in the flowers – and sniffing greedily at the scent. Over the leaves she looked at the man and laughed.

'You are a funny little thing,' said he lazily.

'Why? Because I love flowers?'

'I'd far rather you loved other things,' said the strange man slowly. She broke off a little pink petal and smiled at it.

'Let me send you some flowers,' said the strange man. 'I'll send you a roomful if you'd like them.'

His voice frightened her slightly. 'Oh no, thanks – this one is quite enough for me.'

'No, it isn't' – in a teasing voice.

'What a stupid remark!' thought Viola, and looking at him again he did not seem quite so jolly. She noticed that his eyes were set too closely together – and they were too small. Horrible thought, that he should prove stupid.

'What do you do all day?' she asked hastily.

'Nothing.'

'Nothing at all?'

'Why should I do anything?'

'Oh, don't imagine for one moment that I condemn such wisdom – only it sounds too good to be true!'

'What's that?' – he craned forward. 'What sounds too good to be true?' Yes – there was no denying it – he looked silly.

'I suppose the searching after Fräulein Schäfer doesn't occupy all your days.'

'Oh no' – he smiled broadly – 'that's very good! By Jove! no. I drive a good bit – are you keen on horses?'

She nodded. 'Love them.'

'You must come driving with me – I've got a fine pair of greys. Will you?'

'Pretty I'd look perched behind greys in my one and only

hat,' thought she. Aloud: 'I'd love to.' Her easy acceptance pleased him.

'How about tomorrow?' he suggested. 'Suppose you have lunch with me tomorrow and I take you driving.'

After all – this was just a game. 'Yes, I'm not busy tomorrow,' she said.

A little pause – then the strange man patted his leg. 'Why don't you come and sit down?' he said.

She pretended not to see and swung onto the table. 'Oh, I'm all right here.'

'No, you're not' – again the teasing voice. 'Come and sit on my knee.'

'Oh no,' said Viola very heartily, suddenly busy with her hair.

'Why not?'

'I don't want to.'

'Oh, come along' – impatiently.

She shook her head from side to side. 'I wouldn't dream of such a thing.'

At that he got up and came over to her. 'Funny little puss cat!' He put up one hand to touch her hair.

'Don't,' she said – and slipped off the table. 'I – I think it's time you went now.' She was quite frightened now – thinking only: 'This man must be got rid of as quickly as possible.'

'Oh, but you don't want me to go?'

'Yes, I do – I'm very busy.'

'Busy. What does the pussy cat do all day?'

'Lots and lots of things!' She wanted to push him out of the room and slam the door on him – idiot – fool – cruel disappointment.

'What's she frowning for?' he asked. 'Is she worried about anything?' Suddenly serious: 'I say – you know, are you in any financial difficulty? Do you want money? I'll give it to you if you like!'

'Money! Steady on the brake – don't lose your head!' – so she spoke to herself.

'I'll give you two hundred marks if you'll kiss me.'

'Oh, boo! What a condition! And I don't want to kiss you – I don't like kissing. Please go!'

'Yes – you do! – yes, you do.' He caught hold of her arms above the elbows. She struggled, and was quite amazed to realise how angry she felt.

'Let me go – immediately!' she cried – and he slipped one arm round her body, and drew her towards him – like a bar of iron across her back – that arm.

'Leave me alone! I tell you. Don't be mean! I didn't want this to happen when you came into my room. How dare you?'

'Well, kiss me and I'll go!'

It was too idiotic – dodging that stupid, smiling face.

'I won't kiss you! – you brute! – I won't!' Somehow she slipped out of his arms and ran to the wall – stood back against it – breathing quickly.

'Get out!' she stammered. 'Go on now, clear out!'

At that moment, when he was not touching her, she quite enjoyed herself. She thrilled at her own angry voice. 'To think I should talk to a man like that!' An angry flush spread over his face – his lips curled back, showing his teeth – just like a dog, thought Viola. He made a rush at her, and held her against the wall – pressed upon her with all the weight of his body. This time she could not get free.

'I won't kiss you. I won't. Stop doing that! Ugh! you're like a dog – you ought to find lovers round lamp-posts – you beast – you fiend!'

He did not answer. With an expression of the most absurd

determination he pressed ever more heavily upon her. He did not even look at her – but rapped out in a sharp voice: 'Keep quiet – keep quiet.'

'Gar-r! Why are men so strong?' She began to cry. 'Go away – I don't want you, you dirty creature. I want to murder you. Oh, my God! if I had a knife.'

'Don't be silly – come and be good!' He dragged her towards the bed.

'Do you suppose I'm a light woman?' she snarled, and swooping over she fastened her teeth in his glove.

'*Ach!* don't do that – you are hurting me!'

She did not let go, but her heart said, 'Thank the Lord I thought of this.'

'Stop this minute – you vixen – you bitch.' He threw her away from him. She saw with joy that his eyes were full of tears. 'You've really hurt me,' he said in a choking voice.

'Of course I have. I meant to. That's nothing to what I'll do if you touch me again.'

The strange man picked up his hat. 'No thanks,' he said grimly. 'But I'll not forget this – I'll go to your landlady.'

'Pooh!' She shrugged her shoulders and laughed. 'I'll tell her you forced your way in here and tried to assault me. Who will she believe? – with your bitten hand. You go and find your Schäfers.'

A sensation of glorious, intoxicating happiness flooded Viola. She rolled her eyes at him. 'If you don't go away this moment I'll bite you again,' she said, and the absurd words started her laughing. Even when the door was closed, hearing him descending the stairs, she laughed, and danced about the room.

What a morning! Oh, chalk it up. That was her first fight, and she'd won – she'd conquered that beast – all by herself.

Her hands were still trembling. She pulled up the sleeve of her gown – great red marks on her arms. 'My ribs will be blue. I'll be blue all over,' she reflected. 'If only that beloved Casimir could have seen us.' And the feeling of rage and disgust against Casimir had totally disappeared. How could the poor darling help not having any money? It was her fault as much as his, and he, just like her, was apart from the world, fighting it, just as she had done. If only three o'clock would come. She saw herself running towards him and putting her arms round his neck. 'My blessed one! Of course we are bound to win. Do you love me still? Oh, I have been horrible lately.'

A Blaze

'Max, you silly devil, you'll break your neck if you go careering down the slide that way. Drop it, and come to the Club House with me and get some coffee.'

'I've had enough for today. I'm damp all through. There, give us a cigarette, Victor, old man. When are you going home?'

'Not for another hour. It's fine this afternoon, and I'm getting into decent shape. Look out, get off the track; here comes Fräulein Winkel. Damned elegant the way she manages her sleigh!'

'I'm cold all through. That's the worst of this place – the mists – it's a damp cold. Here, Forman, look after this sleigh – and stick it somewhere so that I can get it without looking through a hundred and fifty others tomorrow morning.'

They sat down at a small round table near the stove and ordered coffee. Victor sprawled in his chair, patting his little brown dog Bobo and looking, half laughingly, at Max.

'What's the matter, my dear? Isn't the world being nice and pretty?'

'I want my coffee, and I want to put my feet into my pocket – they're like stones... Nothing to eat, thanks – the cake is like underdone India rubber here.'

Fuchs and Wistuba came and sat at their table. Max half turned his back and stretched his feet out to the oven. The three other men all began talking at once – of the weather – of the record slide – of the fine condition of the Wald See for skating.

Suddenly Fuchs looked at Max, raised his eyebrows and nodded across to Victor, who shook his head.

'Baby doesn't feel well,' he said, feeding the brown dog with broken lumps of sugar, 'and nobody's to disturb him – I'm nurse.'

'That's the first time I've ever known him off colour,' said Wistuba. 'I've always imagined he had the better part of this world that could not be taken away from him. I think he says his prayers to the dear Lord for having spared him being taken home in seven basketsful tonight. It's a fool's game to risk your all that way and leave the nation desolate.'

'Dry up,' said Max. 'You ought to be wheeled about on the snow in a perambulator.'

'Oh, no offence, I hope. Don't get nasty… How's your wife, Victor?'

'She's not at all well. She hurt her head coming down the slide with Max on Sunday. I told her to stay at home all day.'

'I'm sorry. Are you other fellows going back to the town or stopping on here?'

Fuchs and Victor said they were stopping – Max did not answer, but sat motionless while the men paid for their coffee and moved away. Victor came back a moment and put a hand on his shoulder.

'If you're going right back, my dear, I wish you'd look Elsa up and tell her I won't be in till late. And feed with us tonight at Limpold, will you? And take some hot grog when you get in.'

'Thanks, old fellow, I'm all right. Going back now.'

He rose, stretched himself, buttoned on his heavy coat and lit another cigarette.

From the door Victor watched him plunging through the heavy snow – head bent – hands thrust in his pockets – he almost appeared to be running through the heavy snow towards the town.

Someone came stamping up the stairs – paused at the door of her sitting-room, and knocked.

'Is that you, Victor?' she called.

'No, it is I... can I come in?'

'Of course. Why, what a Santa Claus! Hang your coat on the landing and shake yourself over the banisters. Had a good time?'

The room was full of light and warmth. Elsa, in a white velvet tea-gown, lay curled up on the sofa – a book of fashions on her lap, a box of creams beside her.

The curtains were not yet drawn before the windows and a blue light shone through, and the white boughs of the trees sprayed across.

A woman's room – full of flowers and photographs and silk pillows – the floor smothered in rugs – an immense tiger skin under the piano – just the head protruding – sleepily savage.

'It was good enough,' said Max. 'Victor can't be in till late. He told me to come up and tell you.'

He started walking up and down – tore off his gloves and flung them on the table.

'Don't do that, Max,' said Elsa, 'you get on my nerves. And I've got a headache today; I'm feverish and quite flushed... Don't I look flushed?'

He paused by the window and glanced at her a moment over his shoulder.

'No,' he said; 'I didn't notice it.'

'Oh, you haven't looked at me properly, and I've got a new tea-gown on, too.' She pulled her skirts together and patted a little place on the couch.

'Come along and sit by me and tell me why you're being naughty.'

But, standing by the window, he suddenly flung his arm across his eyes.

'Oh,' he said, 'I can't. I'm done – I'm spent – I'm smashed.'

Silence in the room. The fashion book fell to the floor with a quick rustle of leaves. Elsa sat forward, her hands clasped in her lap; a strange light shone in her eyes, a red colour stained her mouth.

Then she spoke very quietly.

'Come over here and explain yourself. I don't know what on earth you are talking about.'

'You do know – you know far better than I. You've simply played with Victor in my presence that I may feel worse. You've tormented me – you've led me on – offering me everything and nothing at all. It's been a spider-and-fly business from first to last – and I've never for one moment been ignorant of that – and I've never for one moment been able to withstand it.'

He turned round deliberately.

'Do you suppose that when you asked me to pin your flowers into your evening gown – when you let me come into your bedroom when Victor was out while you did your hair – when you pretended to be a baby and let me feed you with grapes – when you have run to me and searched in all my pockets for a cigarette – knowing perfectly well where they were kept – going through every pocket just the same – I knowing too – I keeping up the farce – do you suppose that now you have finally lit your bonfire you are going to find it a peaceful and pleasant thing – you are going to prevent the whole house from burning?'

She suddenly turned white and drew in her breath sharply.

'Don't talk to me like that. You have no right to talk to me like that. I am another man's wife.'

'Hum,' he sneered, throwing back his head, 'that's rather late in the game, and that's been your trump card all along. You only love Victor on the cat-and-cream principle – you a poor little starved kitten that he's given everything to, that he's carried in his breast, never dreaming that those little pink claws could tear out a man's heart.'

She stirred, looking at him with almost fear in her eyes.

'After all' – unsteadily – 'this is my room; I'll have to ask you to go.'

But he stumbled towards her, knelt down by the couch, burying his head in her lap, clasping his arms round her waist.

'And I *love* you – I love you; the humiliation of it – I adore you. Don't – don't – just a minute let me stay here – just a moment in a whole life – Elsa! Elsa!'

She leant back and pressed her head into the pillows.

Then his muffled voice: 'I feel like a savage. I want your whole body. I want to carry you away to a cave and love you until I kill you – you can't understand how a man feels. I kill myself when I see you – I'm sick of my own strength that turns in upon itself, and dies, and rises new-born like a phoenix out of the ashes of that horrible death. Love me just this once, tell me a lie, *say* that you do – you are always lying.'

Instead, she pushed him away – frightened.

'Get up,' she said; 'suppose the servant came in with the tea?'

'Oh, ye gods!' He stumbled to his feet and stood staring down at her.

'You're rotten to the core and so am I. But you're heathenishly beautiful.'

The woman went over to the piano – stood there – striking one note – her brows drawn together. Then she shrugged her shoulders and smiled.

'I'll make a confession. Every word you have said is true. I can't help it. I can't help seeking admiration any more than a cat can help going to people to be stroked. It's my nature. I'm born out of my time. And yet, you know, I'm not a *common* woman. I like men to adore me – to flatter me – even to make love to me – but I would never give myself to any man. I would never let a man kiss me... even.'

'It's immeasurably worse – you've no legitimate excuse. Why, even a prostitute has a greater sense of generosity!'

'I know,' she said, 'I know perfectly well – but I can't help the way I'm built... Are you going?'

He put on his gloves.

'Well,' he said, 'what's going to happen to us now?'

Again she shrugged her shoulders. 'I haven't the slightest idea. I never have – just let things occur.'

'All alone?' cried Victor. 'Has Max been here?'

'He only stayed a moment, and wouldn't even have tea. I sent him home to change his clothes... He was frightfully boring.'

'You poor darling, your hair's coming down. I'll fix it, stand still a moment... so you were bored?'

'Um-m – frightfully... Oh, you've run a hairpin right into your wife's head – you naughty boy!'

She flung her arms round his neck and looked up at him, half laughing, like a beautiful, loving child.

'God! What a woman you are,' said the man. 'You make me so infernally proud – dearest, that I... I tell you!'

NOTES

1. Stomach.
2. *Bon appetit!*
3. Dear lady.
4. Cure.
5. Thus passes the glory of the 'German' world.
6. To use '*du*' – the informal second person pronoun – in addressing a person is to treat them with a degree of informality here apparently viewed as great flattery.
7. Eduard Mörike (1804–75) was a German poet and clergyman.
8. Huge scene!
9. Isn't that right?
10. Oh God!
11. Dear God!
12. In the Homeric tradition of the Trojan War, Patroclus was a friend of Achilles, who was killed by the Trojan prince Hector. The struggle referred to by Doctor Erb is that of the Greeks and Trojans for possession of Patroclus' body.
13. Lord God.
14. 'Oh world, how wonderful you are!'
15. *Hamlet* Act I, scene iii.

BIOGRAPHICAL NOTE

Katherine Mansfield was born in Wellington, New Zealand, in 1888. Her father, Harold Beauchamp, was a successful businessman and was later to become a director of the Bank of New Zealand; her mother, Annie Dyer, a difficult and critical woman, is thought to have provided the model for Mrs Burnell in Mansfield's story 'Prelude'.

At the age of fifteen, Mansfield was sent to be educated at Queen's College, London, where her behaviour marked her out as a non-conformist. In a letter of 1904, she wrote of her disgust at the constraints placed on women and said that she longed for 'power over circumstances'. This moral independence prefigured her attitude to life as well as literature.

In 1908 Mansfield married a singing teacher, George Bowden, though she left him the day after the wedding to resume an affair with another musician, Garnet Trowell. She became pregnant by Trowell and moved, at her mother's insistance, to a guesthouse in Bavaria where the child was stillborn. Her experience was to be used to good effect in her first published work, *In a German Pension* (1911).

The success of this work introduced Mansfield to the London literary scene, and she formed close, if turbulent, friendships with a number of other modernists, in particular D.H. Lawrence and Virginia Woolf, who claimed to be 'jealous' of Mansfield's writing. In 1912, Mansfield met and married the writer John Middleton Murry, with whom she edited a number of literary journals.

The First World War was to be a critical point for the modernist movement, and for Mansfield herself. She wrote of the need to find 'new expressions, new moulds for our new thoughts and feelings'. She also began to write of her homeland, New Zealand – a place of untapped possibility – and here she set some of her most highly regarded stories, including 'Prelude' (1918).

By the end of the war, Mansfield had begun to suffer from tuberculosis. She continued to publish, however, and her collections *Bliss* and *The Garden Party* appeared in 1920 and 1922 respectively. Despite an exhaustive search for a cure, Mansfield died early in 1923, though several stories, as well as letters and journals, were published after her death by Murry.

HESPERUS PRESS – 100 PAGES

Hesperus Press, as suggested by the Latin motto, is committed to bringing near what is far – far both in space and time. Works written by the greatest authors, and unjustly neglected or simply little known in the English-speaking world, are made accessible through new translations and a completely fresh editorial approach. Through these short classic works, each around 100 pages in length, the reader will be introduced to the greatest writers from all times and all cultures.

For more information on Hesperus Press, please visit our website: **www.hesperuspress.com**

ET REMOTISSIMA PROPE